The Time Gates Rebellion

By
Karl-Heinz Schradt

(Schradt'z Artz)
schradtzartz.wordpress.com

Original Draft written in 2006.
Rewritten and edited in 2025

1

A dark reign of one thousand years...

The distant future is bleak. The Kaldrosdom had crushed its enemies with terrifying ease, reigning supreme. The universe's population had fallen victim to a single, mighty invention that cemented the Kaldros's dominance: the Gravatis.

Conceived by Ilores, the Kaldros's dark and brilliant scientist, the Gravatis device defied imagination. It manipulated gravitational forces, rendering traditional fuel-based space travel obsolete. The Kaldros's armies could harness the pull of distant planets, suns, and even black holes to conquer the universe. Entire civilizations crumbled, unable to withstand the Kaldrosdom's might.

2

"The Kaldros does not recognize defeat!" the Monarch thundered.

He stood before the Throne, his robed figure commanding the cavernous hall. The flickering light of torches cast long shadows, and his glowing yellow eyes burned with malice. Before him, Prince Sorrell and General Mardovick knelt on the cold marble floor, their heads bowed in submission.

The silence was oppressive. Along the walls, the Kaldros's elite guard, the Carnos, stood motionless, their armor gleaming like obsidian.

"You," the Kaldros roared, "my chosen leaders, have failed me! You have nothing to fear but the shame of admitting your incompetence!"

The Kaldros descended the stairs, his crimson cape flowing behind him like a river of blood. To his people, he was not just a king but a god in mortal form. His power extended beyond governance—he was the architect of the Time Gates, the master of Gravatis, and the eternal enforcer of Kaldrosdom's rule.

"For a thousand years, I have ruled this universe. I am the suns, the stars, the past, and the future. I am all things to all people!" His voice resonated like thunder, shaking the walls.

Prince Sorrell dared to glance upward, terror etched across his face. In an instant, the Kaldros's hands lashed out, gripping Sorrell and Mardovick by their throats.

"I ordered you to deliver the deaths of the last free rebels," he growled. "Instead, I will deliver yours!"

The two men gasped and clawed at the Kaldros's steely grip, their struggles futile. Their lives were slipping away when a calm, measured voice interrupted.

"My Kaldros."

The Kaldros paused, turning his fiery gaze toward the doorway. A silver figure stood there, draped in royal purple robes. Ilores, the Kaldros's dark scientist, floated into the room, his mechanical frame gleaming.

"Ilores," the Kaldros snarled, his tone a mix of recognition and warning.

Ilores inclined his head. "Your Prince has devised an intriguing strategy."

The Kaldros's eyes flicked to his captives. With a flick of his wrists, he hurled them across the room. They slid to a halt at Ilores's feet, gasping for breath.

"Speak," the Kaldros commanded, ascending the stairs to his throne.

Ilores spread his arms in a sweeping gesture. "Though Prince Sorrell failed to breach the Genowan Solar System, he has secured a meeting."

"A meeting?" the Kaldros repeated, disdain dripping from the words.

"Yes, my Lord. An ambassador from the Genowans will arrive at the Guild of Mars to negotiate... peace." Ilores delivered the word with deliberate precision.

The Kaldros's laughter was sharp and cruel. "Peace?"

Still kneeling, Sorrell found his voice. "The ambassador's trust will be earned, my Kaldros. When they return to Genowan, we will use the opportunity to learn their defenses."

Ilores added, "A drone craft, hidden aboard the ambassador's ship, would gather invaluable intelligence as it navigates their asteroid defenses."

The Kaldros's glowing eyes bore into his son. "And what bargain led to this... opportunity?"

Sorrell's voice wavered. "A Genowan general, from the battle of Taurus. They expect a fair meeting, Father... my Kaldros."

The Kaldros's expression twisted with contempt, but Ilores interjected smoothly. "For the ruse to succeed, the Prince must attend. The Genowans must believe in our sincerity."

The throne room held its breath. Finally, the Kaldros growled, "Sorrell and Mardovick will go to the Guild of Mars. They will either secure victory or meet their end before the next Quantization."

Sorrell bowed stiffly, his neck still aching. "Thank you, my Kaldros." He and Mardovick retreated, the heavy doors closing behind them with a resounding thud.

Ilores floated closer to the throne. "Your grace, Sorrell is far from your strongest warrior, but he may yet prove useful."

The Kaldros's voice was icy. "I do not trust him, Ilores. You will be his shadow."

"As always, I am yours to command," Ilores replied, bowing deeply.

3

A hundred starships or more, each emblazoned with the Kaldros's seal, surged through the void of space toward Mars. Traveling at speeds far beyond the comprehension of most, they carved glowing trails across the darkness, like harbingers of destruction. At the heart of the fleet, aboard the command ship, Prince Sorrell and General Mardovick stood on the bridge.

Sorrell's hand lingered on the bruises encircling his neck, the marks of his father's wrath still raw. He winced as the pain flared anew.

"What say you, Mardovick?" he asked, his tone sharp despite the injury.

The seasoned general turned to face the Prince, his features shadowed by years of war and service. Once a member of the elite Carnos, he had since traded his ceremonial armor for the mantle of leadership over the Kaldros's armies.

"Our time grows short, my Prince," Mardovick replied, his voice low and gravelly. "The Kaldros will not accept further failure. He will demand results."

Sorrell's lips curved into a thin smile, though his eyes betrayed no amusement. "This plan will gain us time. I will tell my father that the dronecraft's data is promising but complex. That will delay his expectations."

He crossed his arms and stared out at the stars beyond the ship's viewing pane. "Our mining operation on Jupiter has given us the capital we need. Soon, we'll have the armies to hold the palace and destroy the Time Gates, should it come to that. The Royal Armies will follow my command long enough for us to secure our position."

"The plan hinges on the Genowan ambassador returning the dronecraft to Genowan," Mardovick said, his tone laced with caution.

Sorrell turned, a glimmer of confidence in his eyes. "He will. And to ensure it, I have a gift that will make him trust me."

Mardovick's brow furrowed. "A gift?"

Sorrell's sly smile widened. "Gravatis."

The general's eyes widened in disbelief. "You're giving the Genowans Gravatis?"

"Not entirely," Sorrell replied. "When the Genowans integrate Gravatis into their fleets, it will disrupt the Kaldrosdom's balance. Chaos will ensue, and in that chaos, we'll find our opportunity to unseat my father. We can bring sanity to this universe."

Mardovick's expression remained grim, but he nodded. "As you wish, my Prince."

4

Act I: The Tralonu Destiny

Theresa Manak stood at the window of her small home in San Gimignano, staring out at the silhouette of the town's medieval towers. The summer night was stifling, and she had opened the window to let a faint breeze in for her sleeping baby, Shania.

Even in the darkness, the shapes of the ancient towers were distinct against the starry sky. Life in this quiet Tuscan town had been kind to her. She and her husband, Vandar, ran a modest shop together, a far cry from the life they had left behind.

Vandar stirred in his sleep, the sheets tangled around him. To Theresa, it seemed like any other restless night. But within Vandar's mind, old memories surfaced like dark waves crashing against a fragile shore.

Sarus Danak, commander of the Fifth Fleet's garrisons, stood at the podium in the stormtroopers' briefing room. Before him stretched a sea of armored soldiers, their black uniforms shining under the harsh lights. They stood at rigid attention, awaiting his command.

Sarus removed his helmet, revealing a face hardened by years of war. His piercing gaze swept across the room, and his voice boomed with authority.

"The people you encounter are traitors. Show them no mercy," he declared.

A murmur rippled through the assembled troops, their anticipation palpable.

"All who defy the Kaldrosdom—no matter their age, gender, or station—must be eradicated. They threaten the rule of the Kaldros and the safety of his subjects." He raised a fist, his voice growing louder. "They will be annihilated!"

The soldiers roared in response, their voices a thunderous echo of the commander's rage.

Moments later, the fleet's largest transport ship touched down on the outskirts of Balzac City, a mining colony on the young planet Ethsiz. The city, a cluster of industrial buildings, was surrounded on all sides by the Kaldros's forces.

Vandar Manak, now a squadron leader, rode in the first wave of transports. Through the visor of his helmet, he scanned his soldiers. Their faces were obscured, their loyalty absolute. Vandar himself had once been no different.

"Do we hold until the target is confirmed?" his communications officer, Tharon, asked.

"No," Vandar replied coldly. "You heard the orders. If they're not ours, kill them."

The transports rumbled into the city square, meeting sporadic resistance. Civilians screamed and scattered as stormtroopers marched forward. Snipers fired from windows, but their efforts were futile. The Kaldros's forces crushed all opposition with ruthless efficiency.

Suddenly, a massive explosion rocked the square. Vandar turned to see one of the transports reduced to a flaming wreck.

"Take cover!" he shouted, leading his men to shelter behind a subway entrance.

Laser fire rained down from the surrounding buildings. Several soldiers fell, their armor no match for the onslaught. Vandar scanned the upper floors, his targeting system searching for enemies.

Then he saw them: six figures shrouded in green light, floating effortlessly through the smoky air. The Carnos.

The Kaldros's elite bodyguards moved like phantoms, their black capes billowing as fiery orbs formed above their palms. Without a word, the orbs streaked toward the snipers, exploding on impact and engulfing entire floors in flames.

Vandar watched in awe as the Carnos methodically obliterated the enemy. Their shields absorbed every shot, their movements impossibly fast. Within moments, the resistance was quelled. The buildings crackled with fire, and the screams of the wounded faded into silence.

5

The blockade at the building's entrance was obliterated in seconds, Vandar's explosives reducing it to a heap of smoking rubble. He and his unit stormed through, blasters raised, moving with precision honed by years of combat. The rebel stronghold was a maze of tight corridors and makeshift barricades, but their mission was simple: eliminate everyone.

The assault lasted four grueling days. Explosions rocked the city as guerrilla warfare consumed every street and building. For Vandar, every kill brought satisfaction—a traitor's life extinguished, one less threat to the Kaldrosdom. By the end, the resistance was broken, reduced to scattered survivors making futile last stands.

Vandar's final kill on Ethsiz was seared into his memory. His unit was returning to their transport, the mission complete, when a noise stopped him. He turned, blaster raised, as a figure emerged from the rubble of a collapsed apartment block. A girl, no older than seventeen, stumbled toward him. Her hair was matted with blood and ash, her face streaked with soot. She screamed, her voice cracking with grief and rage.

"You killed him!" she shrieked, her steps faltering as tears streamed down her face. "My little brother—you bastards, you killed him!"

Vandar didn't hesitate. She was unarmed, hysterical, and an easy target. He waited just long enough for her to finish her sentence, then fired a single, perfect shot. She fell, disappearing into the ruins.

He approached the body, scanning the rubble until he found her. Her eyes were wide, her expression frozen in anguish. Vandar felt nothing. He sneered inwardly, thinking, *At least she got to say her piece.*

In his dream, the scene replayed, but this time it was different. He wasn't the hardened soldier anymore—he was himself, as he was now. The realization hit him like a tidal wave. He gasped for air, his chest tightening as if an iron grip held him. He collapsed to his knees, bile rising in his throat. The faces of the people he'd killed flooded his mind. Their screams filled his ears, drowning out everything else.

He clawed at his chest, desperate to rid himself of the evil he felt coursing through him. *I don't deserve this life,* he thought. *I'm a monster.*

His comrades in the dream rushed to his side, shouting in confusion.

"What's wrong with him?" one yelled.

"He's lost it!" another cried, panic in his voice.

Vandar screamed, his voice raw and ragged. Their hands grabbed at him, trying to restrain him, but he didn't fight back. He didn't care. All he wanted was to be destroyed, to erase himself from existence.

Vandar woke with a gasp, his heart pounding. The sunlight streaming through the window felt wrong—too bright, too warm. He sat up, struggling to catch his breath. Slowly, the sounds of morning seeped in: birds chirping outside, the faint creak of the house settling. He wasn't on Ethsiz. He was home.

"Theresa?" he called, his voice shaky.

She appeared in the doorway, her brow furrowed with concern. "Vandar, are you okay? You look terrible."

He ran a hand through his damp hair. "I didn't sleep well," he admitted.

Theresa sat beside him, taking his hand. "I noticed. I went to check on Shania around one in the morning, and you were thrashing in your sleep."

He sighed, leaning back against the headboard. "It was the dreams again. The past."

Her hand stroked his hair gently. "You're not that man anymore," she said softly. "That life is behind you now."

He looked at her, her serene smile grounding him. The warmth of her touch eased the knot in his chest. For a moment, he allowed himself to believe her.

"Well," she added with a teasing grin, "the good news is it's the weekend."

Vandar chuckled, some of the tension leaving his shoulders. "Does it really count as a weekend if I have to see your dad?"

Theresa smirked. "Yes, it does. And you're the one who can explain everything best. He respects you. Plus, he loves technical talk—he'll follow the science."

"Lucky me," Vandar said, leaning in to kiss her. "I'll make it work."

As he dressed, the remnants of his dream lingered, but he pushed them aside. He couldn't change the past, but his future—with Theresa and Shania—was something he could protect. And that made all the difference.

6

It was the end of a tranquil day in Arezzo, a picturesque town nestled in the Tuscan hills. The winter sky was ablaze with crimson and gold as the sun sank below the horizon. Vandar walked through the narrow, cobblestone streets, the air cool and tinged with the faint aroma of wood smoke. He stopped in front of the villa of his father-in-law, Signore Gino Forlanini, a retired English lecturer known for his sharp wit and love of philosophy.

Gino, the father of Vandar's wife, Theresa, was a man who valued tradition but relished a good debate. Vandar and Theresa had been married for years and were blessed with a daughter, Shania. Tonight, however, Vandar arrived alone. He was invited onto a small veranda just big enough for two chairs. It overlooked a lively piazza, where townsfolk lingered in the last light of day.

Gino poured a glass of wine and settled into his worn wooden stool, lighting a cigarette with practised ease. His weathered face broke into a sly grin as he addressed his son-in-law.

"You've come alone, Vandar. Where are Theresa and little Shania?"

"They're waiting for me in San Gimignano," Vandar replied, his voice steady yet burdened. "I came alone because there's something I need to say to you. Theresa thought it was important."

Gino raised an eyebrow, his curiosity piqued. "An important message, delivered in person. Intriguing. I'm an old man, Vandar. Say what you must quickly—before I keel over and take your words to the grave!" He chuckled, but the humour faded as he noticed Vandar's sombre expression.

"This isn't an easy conversation, Gino. But I need you to listen carefully."

The older man exhaled a plume of smoke, his gaze sharp. He gestured with his hand, inviting Vandar to continue.

"You've probably thought of me as eccentric," Vandar began, a faint smile tugging at his lips. "Perhaps even a little mad."

"Certainly not without reason," Gino quipped, his grin returning.

Vandar looked out at the piazza below, where the fading daylight cast long shadows. "What I'm about to tell you may seem like proof of that belief. But I assure you, it's no whimsy. It's truth. And Theresa insisted you had a right to know."

Gino's grin faded as he leaned forward, his curiosity giving way to cautious attention.

Vandar took a deep breath. "Most people accept the future as unpredictable, shaped by random events and chance. But I know otherwise."

The old man tilted his head, skepticism flickering in his eyes.

"I've seen the centuries ahead," Vandar said. His tone was calm, but his words carried weight. "And before I explain what awaits, I need to tell you why I know it to be certain."

Gino stubbed out his cigarette, giving his son-in-law his full attention.

"First, a refresher on gravity," Vandar began. "It's the force that pulls objects together. It keeps us on this planet, binds the moon in its orbit, and shapes the cosmos. Some even believe it will bring about the universe's end."

Gino nodded, his intellect engaged. "And time?"

"Time is more elusive," Vandar said, his voice growing quieter. "Though it seems constant in our daily lives, it bends under the influence of gravity, as Einstein described. And at extreme speeds, time becomes... malleable."

Vandar leaned forward, his tone intensifying. "Travel fast enough, and time slows for the traveler while the universe moves on. Travel even faster, and time for the universe stops. Push beyond that, and time reverses."

Gino gave a skeptical laugh. "So, you're telling me you've traveled to the future?"

Vandar raised a hand, his eyes serious. "Hear me out. The key isn't speed alone—it's gravity. With control over gravity, speed becomes limitless. And with speed, time becomes a tool—not a boundary."

Vandar gestured toward the coffee table, picking up an apple. "Take this apple. Gravity pulls it down, as it did for Newton. But what if I could make it fall upward?"

He dropped the apple, and it thudded onto the wooden floor. "Now imagine replacing this apple with a spacecraft. With control over gravity, it could 'fall' not just upward but through the vast expanse of space, accelerating past light speed."

Gino folded his arms, his expression guarded.

Vandar met his gaze, his voice dropping to a near whisper. "This isn't theoretical. It's real. And it's already been done. But here's the truth you need to understand: everything today is a consequence of yesterday. The future depends on the past staying exactly as it is."

"What are you saying, Vandar?" Gino asked, his voice low.

Vandar straightened, his face grave. "We are in the past, Gino. Our future descendants are holding us here—trapped in time. They control the past to secure their existence."

Gino sat back, his cigarette forgotten. "Why? Why meddle with what's done?"

Vandar looked away, his voice heavy with regret. "Because the only threat to the future is the past."

Gino's hands tightened around his glass, his thoughts racing. "If I trust you, what must I do?"

Vandar extended a hand. "Pack your things. Come with me. There's no going back if you do. Theresa wanted you to have this choice."

After a long pause, Gino slapped Vandar on the arm, a grin spreading across his face. "I'm old, Vandar. I need an adventure. Lead the way."

Vandar grinned back. "We leave for San Gimignano tonight. From there—London."

And with that, the two men stepped into the unknown.

7

The drive to San Gimignano was swift, and Gino's mood lightened as he reunited with Theresa and his infant granddaughter, Shania. His face softened as he cradled the baby in his arms, marveling at her wide-eyed innocence. Yet beneath his jovial exterior, Vandar noticed a flicker of hesitation in the old man's eyes—a silent recognition of the life he was about to leave behind.

From San Gimignano, they drove to Pisa to catch a late-night flight to London. The transition felt surreal, as though the familiar landmarks of Tuscany were slipping away like grains of sand through an hourglass. At the airport, Gino lingered by a café window, his gaze fixed on the rolling hills in the distance, before Theresa gently ushered him onward.

The family spent the night at a modest hotel near Heathrow. The following morning, the quiet hum of city life seeped into their breakfast conversation as Vandar laid out the next step of their journey.

"We'll need to hire a car and drive out of London to Stonehenge," he said, his voice clipped with purpose.

Gino, stirring sugar into his espresso, nodded casually. "That's fine. But I'd like to make a brief stop in Central London first. There's something I need to take care of."

Vandar paused, his spoon hovering mid-air over his coffee. "What could be so important? You do understand, Gino—you're leaving your life behind. After this, nothing about your world will remain the same."

"I haven't forgotten," Gino replied, his tone light. "It's just a quick stop. There's a language institute I've been working with. I was supposed to finalize a contract to edit their next Italian language book."

Vandar sighed, running a hand through his hair. Before he could respond, Theresa intervened, her voice calm but firm.

"Father," she said, setting down her teacup, "after you come with us, you'll no longer exist in the timeline as it is now. Anything you do —this book, this contract—it will all disappear by the next New Year. The Time Gates will erase your presence."

Gino furrowed his brow, the weight of her words settling over him. "Erase?" he echoed.

"Once you pass through the gates, you're essentially removed from history as far as it's recorded," Theresa explained, glancing at Vandar. "If you stay behind after Stonehenge, you'll reintegrate into the timeline. But until then, nothing you do will have any lasting impact."

Gino chuckled, a hint of defiance in his tone. "Well, isn't that something. But I've always found editing a language book to be quite a satisfying exercise. If it's all the same to you, I'd like to finish what I started."

Vandar leaned back in his chair, exhaling heavily. "Fine," he said at last. "We'll go to the institute. But after that, no more detours."

A short drive later, they entered Central London, its streets bustling with early-morning energy. The car stopped outside a stately Victorian building with ornate brickwork and tall windows that reflected the gray sky. A brass plaque beside the door read, The Language Teachers Institute.

"This is it," Gino announced, his excitement barely contained. "Care to join me?"

Theresa shook her head, adjusting Shania's baby carrier. "I'll stay here. Maybe take Shania for a walk. Vandar, you go with him."

Vandar hesitated but eventually followed the older man. Gino climbed the steep stone steps slowly, steadying himself on the railing. Vandar, noticing the strain on his father-in-law's face, reached out. "Here, let me take the briefcase."

"Thank you," Gino said, flashing a grateful smile. "Age catches up with us all, doesn't it?"

Inside, the reception area was warm and welcoming, its walls adorned with maps and posters of European landmarks. A cheerful receptionist greeted them.

"Seniore Forlanini!" she exclaimed, her eyes lighting up. "What a pleasure to meet you in person."

"The pleasure is mine," Gino replied, his tone as bright as the woman's smile.

"If you have a moment, Mister Walker would be happy to see you," she added.

They were soon ushered into a cozy office where Mister Walker, the institute's general manager, greeted them with enthusiasm. The room smelled faintly of leather and old paper, its shelves lined with language textbooks.

"Seniore Forlanini, we're thrilled to have you on board for this project," Walker said, shaking his hand warmly.

"And I'm delighted to be part of it," Gino replied, his voice carrying genuine pride.

Walker glanced at Vandar. "And you must be—?"

"My son-in-law," Gino said. "Vandar Manak."

Walker studied Vandar for a moment, curiosity flickering in his eyes. "Manak... an unusual name. Eastern European?"

Vandar hesitated, then nodded. "Something like that."

Walker seemed satisfied, turning his attention back to Gino. "Well, Seniore Forlanini, everything seems to be in order. If you'll sign here, we'll send the first manuscripts to your Arezzo address by March."

Gino signed the contract with deliberate care, his pen scratching across the paper. For a brief moment, he seemed lost in thought, his fingers lingering on the final page.

As they descended the stairs, Gino stopped abruptly. "You know," he said, glancing back at Vandar, "this book might never see the light of day. But it feels good to leave something behind—even if it's just for myself."

Vandar frowned but said nothing.

Back at the car, Theresa asked, "How did it go?"

"Very well," Gino replied, his face alight with satisfaction. "It's a good project. A fine opportunity."

Vandar glanced at her and Shania, who gurgled contentedly in her mother's arms. "The people there seemed nice enough," he said. "It's a shame it'll all... disappear."

As they drove away from the city, the bustling streets gave way to the quiet expanse of the English countryside. Gino sat silently, gazing out the window as though committing every detail to memory.

"Wait!" he suddenly exclaimed. "I left my briefcase at the institute!"

Vandar sighed, shaking his head. "We'll pick it up on the way back," he said, his voice resigned.

Theresa chuckled softly, patting Vandar's arm. "He's still attached to the little things," she said.

As the car sped toward Stonehenge, the horizon stretched wide and unbroken, a reminder of the unknown that lay ahead.

8

The frosty English countryside unfolded like a watercolor painting, mist clinging to the fields and frost sparkling on the grass under a pale winter sun. Gino watched the scenery with interest, the unfamiliar chill biting through his coat. England was starkly different from Tuscany—colder, more subdued—but beautiful in its own way. His thoughts, however, were far from the landscape.

In the back seat, Theresa cradled Shania, who had fallen peacefully asleep after her milk. Vandar glanced at them through the rearview mirror. Theresa's long dark hair framed her serene expression, and Shania's tiny hand rested on her mother's chest. Vandar's heart swelled as he thought about how much they had changed his life. Before them, he'd been unmoored, drifting through life without purpose. Now, they were his world. He couldn't lose them.

Theresa broke the silence. "I'm sorry I didn't explain everything to you myself, Dad. I didn't think I could make you understand."

Gino gave a soft chuckle, though his eyes stayed on the passing fields. "I'm not sure I understand even now."

"I'm glad you're here," Theresa said, touching his arm with a gentle smile.

Gino smiled back. "So, where are we headed?"

Vandar spoke without looking away from the road. "We're driving to the ley lines near Stonehenge. It's one of the most powerful intersections in the world."

Gino raised an eyebrow. "Ley lines? What exactly are those?"

Vandar hesitated, as if searching for the simplest explanation. "Think of them as pathways of energy. Just like gravity creates patterns in the universe, these lines mirror those patterns on Earth. They're places where the forces of the universe behave differently."

"As on Earth, so it is in the heavens," Gino murmured, recalling the words of his Sunday prayers from decades ago.

Vandar nodded. "Exactly. We need to position ourselves on the ley lines before midnight on New Year's Eve. That's when the Time Gates reset history."

Theresa added, "At midnight, the gates perform something called the Quantisation. They align the past with the universe's intended history, correcting any anomalies."

Gino smirked. "So we're spending New Year's Eve in the middle of a field, hiding from... what? Cosmic accountants?"

Vandar allowed a faint smile but stayed focused on the road. "It's not just about the Quantisation. The ley lines are the only places immune to the gates' effects, but that also makes them dangerous. They're often guarded."

Gino stiffened. "Guarded? By who?"

"The Carnos," Vandar replied. "They're law-keepers for the Time Gates. They patrol every New Year's Eve throughout history, watching for anomalies like us."

Gino turned in his seat to face him. "And you think risking Theresa and Shania is worth this madness?"

Vandar met Gino's gaze briefly in the mirror. "If we don't, Shania will cease to exist. Theresa won't remember me. And you—you'll forget all of this ever happened."

Gino stared at him, stunned. "Cease to exist?" he repeated, his voice rising. "I love my family. I won't let that happen."

Theresa reached out to take her father's hand. "I know it's hard to believe, Dad. But please, trust us."

For a moment, Gino said nothing, his thoughts a whirlwind of confusion and disbelief. Finally, he sighed, looking out at the frost-covered fields. "Madness," he muttered. "Pure madness."

9

The stark silhouette of Stonehenge rose before them, its ancient stones bathed in the pale light of a cloudy afternoon. Gino felt a momentary awe as he walked among the massive monoliths, pushing Shania's pram over the uneven ground. The baby cooed happily, her joy infectious, and for a while, Gino allowed himself to focus on her rather than the strange circumstances that had brought them here.

Vandar and Theresa lagged behind, poring over a map and speaking in hushed tones. Gino glanced back at them occasionally, watching his son-in-law with a mix of curiosity and skepticism. Vandar seemed focused—too focused—and it unsettled him.

"What's your daddy doing, Shania?" Gino asked the baby as he glanced toward Vandar.

Shania babbled in response, waving her tiny fists. Gino followed her gaze to where Vandar now stood alone, eyes closed, clutching his peculiar metal bracelet. He stayed like that for minutes, motionless, as if communing with the ancient stones.

"Ha perso le retelle," Gino muttered to himself, shaking his head. "He's lost the plot."

When they regrouped at the exit, Theresa smiled as she took Shania into her arms. Vandar, still preoccupied, glanced back at the stones with an intensity that unsettled Gino.

"I think I've found the right spot," Vandar said. "We'll need to wait until midnight tomorrow."

"Any hotel nearby will do for now," Theresa said, eager to rest.
Gino nodded, relieved. "Finally, some sense."

10

The last light of New Year's Eve faded into the horizon as they parked on a desolate country road. The chill of the winter evening crept through the air, biting at their faces as they stepped out into the gathering darkness. The silence of the countryside was profound, broken only by the crunch of their footsteps on frost-covered grass.

Vandar led the way, holding Shania's small bag slung over one shoulder and the strange metal bracelet clutched tightly in his hand. Behind him, Theresa cradled Shania, who had fallen asleep despite the cold, while Gino trudged along, his eyes darting nervously to the shadows that flitted among the trees.

"Why does he keep holding that thing?" Gino muttered to himself, watching Vandar glance down at the bracelet every few steps. He made a mental note to ask about it later—assuming there was a later.

They emerged from the forest into an open field. The mist clung low to the ground, obscuring the contours of the land and swallowing any sign of distant hills. Vandar stopped abruptly and turned to the others, pointing toward a cluster of willows by a shallow river.

"There," he said. "We'll stay under the trees."

The final rays of twilight faded as they reached the grove. Vandar turned off the flashlight, plunging them into darkness. When they looked up, they were met with a breathtaking sight. The night sky stretched above them in pristine clarity, the Milky Way blazing a brilliant trail across the heavens.

For a moment, even Gino was struck speechless.

"What now?" he finally whispered, his voice barely carrying over the soft rustle of the breeze.

Vandar's face was grave as he spoke. "We stay here. Don't move. Don't make a sound. If we're seen, it could mean the end for all of us."

"Seen by who?" Gino asked, his breath visible in the cold air.

"The ley lines are guarded," Vandar replied quietly. "By the Carnos."

Gino's brow furrowed. "The who?"

"The Carnos," Vandar said again. "Sworn law-keepers of the Time Gates. They patrol every New Year's Eve, across every year of history, searching for anomalies like us—those trying to escape the reset."

Gino shook his head in disbelief. "And here I thought you were the madman in this family," he muttered, glancing at Theresa. "Now I see it runs in the blood."

Theresa ignored his remark, her voice calm but firm. "Papa, just listen to Vandar. Please."

Gino sighed, crouching behind the thick trunk of a willow tree. Theresa curled protectively around Shania, holding her close to shield her from the cold. Vandar stood a short distance away, glancing between the bracelet in his hand and the watch on his wrist.

"Five minutes," he said under his breath.

A distant pop echoed through the air—fireworks from some nearby village. The faint glow of sparks briefly illuminated the horizon before fading into darkness.

Vandar tensed. "One minute," he whispered.

The air grew heavy, and a low hum began to resonate through the ground. Gino clung to the rough bark of the tree as the stars above seemed to shift, their brightness intensifying until the night sky looked alive. The Milky Way spun faster, its stars streaking into long trails of colored light that swirled like a cosmic whirlpool.

"Look," Vandar whispered, pointing upward.

The heavens themselves appeared to break apart. Light cascaded from the sky in shimmering ribbons, illuminating the grove in hues of gold, blue, and green. The ground beneath them trembled as the wind whipped through the trees, carrying with it a sound like distant thunder. Gino's heart pounded as he watched, torn between awe and terror.

Then came the light.

A sharp, green glow pierced through the swirling chaos, emanating from the far side of the grove. Vandar stiffened, his body rigid with tension. He turned toward the source, his face grim.

"It's here," he muttered.

From the center of the glow, a figure emerged. It floated just above the ground, its form clad in armor that seemed to radiate its own light. The armor resembled that of a medieval knight, but it was impossibly sleek, its surface etched with glowing lines that pulsed faintly. The figure was massive—at least seven feet tall—and moved with an eerie, deliberate grace.

Above its outstretched hands hovered two orbs of fire, their orange glow casting flickering shadows across the trees.

Vandar gritted his teeth. "Stay hidden," he hissed.

The Carnos drifted closer, scanning the grove. Its glowing eyes swept methodically through the darkness, searching. Vandar knew it wouldn't be long before they were found. He glanced at Theresa, who clutched Shania tightly, her face pale but composed. Gino, on the other hand, was frozen in terror, his wide eyes locked on the advancing figure.

Vandar reached into his bag, pulling out a pistol-like weapon. He took a deep breath, steeling himself. Then, with a yell, he leapt from behind the tree and fired.

The blast struck the Carnos square in the chest, sending it hurtling backward. It recovered almost instantly, its fiery orbs flaring as it turned its glowing eyes on Vandar. With a sweep of its arms, the orbs shot forward, streaking through the air like flaming meteors.

Vandar dove to the side as the orbs smashed into the ground where he'd stood, sending a shower of dirt and sparks into the air. He rolled to his feet just in time to see the Carnos charging toward him, a glowing sword drawn from its back.

He fired again—two shots deflected by the Carnos' sword in brilliant bursts of light. The third shot found its mark, striking the center of its helmet. The creature froze mid-step, its glowing eyes flickering before fading entirely. With a metallic groan, it collapsed to the ground, its fiery orbs sputtering out like dying embers.

Vandar lowered his weapon, his chest heaving. For a moment, he simply stood there, staring at the darkened armor.

"Theresa!" he called, turning toward the grove.

She emerged cautiously, Shania still in her arms. "We're okay," she said, her voice trembling slightly. "Are you?"

Vandar nodded, pulling her into an embrace. "Gino?" he called.

From behind a tree, Gino staggered out, his face pale and his hands trembling. "I'm here," he rasped. "I... I think I'm okay."

Vandar let out a breath of relief. "We have to go," he said. "Now."

The car sped through the darkness, the tension inside palpable. Gino sat in silence, his hands gripping his knees. Theresa hummed softly to calm Shania, who had woken during the chaos.

"Are we safe now?" Gino finally asked.

Vandar didn't take his eyes off the road. "We're safe for now. But when the Carnos doesn't report back, others will come. We need to stay off their radar."

Theresa frowned. "And next year?"

Vandar hesitated. "We can't return to the same ley lines. It's too dangerous. They'll be waiting for us."

"Next year?" Gino repeated, slumping in his seat. "You mean we'll have to do this all over again?"

Vandar glanced at him in the rearview mirror. "Until the Time Gates no longer control us, we're fugitives. This is the only way."

Gino said nothing, the weight of the night settling over him like a shroud.

11

The trip back to London was cloaked in silence. The car's engine hummed softly as the suburbs of the city began to emerge in the distance, their warm lights casting faint glows on the frost-covered streets. Gino stared out the window, his thoughts a chaotic blur, his jaw clenched in frustration. He didn't speak until the familiar outline of the language institute came into view.

"Can we stop here? I need to pick up my briefcase," he said, his voice low and tense.

Vandar gave a slight nod, saying nothing as he pulled into the same parking spot. Gino stepped out, his movements heavy, and climbed the stairs without waiting for an offer of help.

From the driver's seat, Vandar watched him go. "He's not taking this well," he said, breaking the silence.

Theresa sighed, her gaze lingering on the building. "It's a lot to process," she replied. "I took time too. He'll come around once he starts to understand the freedom we've gained."

Vandar opened the door and got out, glancing up the stairs. "Should I go after him?"

She hesitated, then nodded. "You should. He may not ask for help, but he needs it."

Gino reached the reception desk, where the young receptionist greeted him with a practiced smile. Her bright ruby lipstick seemed almost garish against the building's stark lighting.

"Yes, we were hoping you'd come back," she said, reaching under the desk to retrieve his briefcase.

"Thank you," Gino said stiffly, taking it from her.

At that moment, Vandar appeared behind him. Gino tensed but didn't turn around. As if sensing the tension, the institute's manager, Mr. Walker, stepped out of his office with a jovial smile.

"Ah, Senoire Forlanini!" he exclaimed. "Happy New Year! I trust you've come for your briefcase?"

"Yes, happy New Year," Gino replied, his politeness strained. "And yes, I have it now."

"You got everything?" Vandar asked softly.

Gino glanced inside the briefcase, nodding. "No problems."

Walker's gaze shifted to Vandar, curiosity flickering in his eyes. "Is this your son, Senoire Forlanini?"

"No," Gino replied, forcing a smile. "My son-in-law."

Walker blinked in surprise. "I didn't know you had a daughter."

"You met Vandar on the 31st," Gino said. "We came in together."

Walker's smile faltered, replaced by a look of confusion. "I'm sorry, but you were alone."

"Alone?" Gino echoed, his voice rising.

"Yes," Walker said, nodding firmly. The receptionist chimed in with agreement.

"It was just you," she said.

"No, no," Gino said, his voice trembling with disbelief. "Vandar was with me. We spoke to you in your office. You even asked him where he met my daughter!"

Walker exchanged an uncertain glance with the receptionist before turning back to Gino. "I'm sorry, Senoire Forlanini, but I don't recall that at all."

Gino turned to Vandar, his expression a mix of anger and betrayal. Vandar shrugged helplessly.

"Well," Gino said tightly, "I'll be on my way."

Clutching his briefcase, he walked past Vandar and out of the building without another word.

The moment Gino slammed the car door, the tension erupted.

"What the hell was that?" he yelled, his face red with frustration.

"What's going on?"

Theresa turned in her seat, startled. "What's wrong?"

Vandar remained calm, glancing at her. "He's just seen the effects of the Time Gates."

"What are you talking about?" Gino shouted, his voice shaking. "Those two—Walker and that receptionist—they're crazy! They met Vandar, but now they're acting like he doesn't exist!"

Theresa reached out and placed a hand on her father's arm. "Papa, please. Let me explain."

"Explain what?" Gino snapped. "That I'm losing my mind?"

"No," she said firmly. "They can't remember Vandar because, to them, he doesn't exist in the year that's just passed."

"Doesn't exist?" Gino repeated, his voice trembling. "How is that even possible?"

She took a deep breath, her voice calm and measured. "The Time Gates reset history every New Year's Eve. They restore the timeline to how it 'should' have been, according to their design. Anything outside of that—like Vandar being in that office—is erased."

Gino stared at her, his confusion turning to anger. "So none of this happened? Is that what you're saying?"

"It happened," Vandar interjected. "But only to us. To the rest of the world, it didn't."

Theresa leaned forward, her tone softening. "In the original version of 1994, Papa, you didn't come to London. You didn't meet Vandar. You spent New Year's Eve in Arezzo, drinking wine and dancing in the piazza. That's the version of history the Time Gates restored."

Gino slumped back in his seat, his head in his hands. "This is insane. Completely insane."

Vandar's voice was calm but firm. "You're an anomaly now, Gino. Like us. Living outside the Time Gates' control."

Gino suddenly straightened, his eyes blazing. "So now I don't even belong to 1994? Fine! Just fine! Why didn't you warn me about this earlier?"

Before Vandar could respond, Gino threw open the car door and stormed out, narrowly avoiding an oncoming car. He stomped down the street, muttering curses under his breath.

"Damn it!" Vandar muttered, gripping the steering wheel.

"Give him space," Theresa said quietly, her hand on his shoulder. "He needs time to process."

Vandar shook his head. "We can't leave him wandering around. If he talks to the wrong person, the Carnos could find us."

Theresa sighed. "You're right. Go after him. I'll stay here."

Vandar nodded, quickly getting out of the car. He jogged after Gino, who had entered the sprawling expanse of Richmond Park, his dark figure silhouetted against the misty evening light.

Gino wandered through the park, his footsteps heavy. His thoughts raced, bouncing between anger, disbelief, and fear. Finally, he stopped beneath a towering oak, pressing his forehead against the rough bark.

"What's happening to me?" he whispered, his voice barely audible.

Vandar approached cautiously, his own breath visible in the cold air. He didn't speak at first, giving Gino the space to vent his frustration. Finally, he stepped closer, his voice calm but resolute.

"I know how you feel, Gino. I've been there."

Gino didn't respond, but Vandar pressed on. "Your world feels like it's falling apart because it's not what you thought it was. I know how disorienting that is. But it's also an opportunity."

Gino turned his head slightly, his eyes narrowed. "An opportunity? For what?"

Vandar stepped closer, his expression earnest. "To live outside their control. To be free. But I need you to trust me. I need your help."

Gino finally turned to face him, his anger softening into wary curiosity. "Am I free now?" he asked quietly. "Free from the Time Gates?"

Vandar looked away, his voice heavy with regret. "Not yet. But we're working on it."

12

The summer had been warm and balmy, even here in the foothills of the Alps. The Austrian countryside stretched out before them, a serene patchwork of green pastures and dense forests. Gino's command of German had proved invaluable in helping them find this secluded farmhouse, far removed from the highways and tourist crowds heading to Neuschwanstein Castle. The days had been almost cloudless and dry, with the world around them exuding a deceptive calmness.

Gino maneuvered the old tractor into the clearing and stopped it beside the deep circular ditches they had dug. The ditches, concentric rings like the markings of a dartboard or spiderweb, were already bordered by boulders of various sizes and shapes. The trailer behind the tractor carried a single marble boulder, the last piece of the arrangement. He turned off the engine, climbed down, and wiped his brow before walking to inspect the boulder.

"Hey! Don't even think about moving that by yourself, old timer!" came Vandar's voice from the woods.

Gino looked up and saw Vandar and Theresa approaching. Vandar was pushing a wheelbarrow, while Theresa guided Shania's pram beside him. The nearly two-year-old giggled and pointed at the scene, her dark eyes sparkling.

"Why not?" Gino replied, laughing. "The fresh air has done me good—I feel ten years younger!"

Vandar smirked as he parked the wheelbarrow next to the trailer. "Maybe so, but we need these rocks placed perfectly. No shortcuts, Gino."

Gino chuckled and stepped down from the trailer, shaking his head. "You're the boss, son," he said with a mock bow, walking over to the pram. He knelt to greet Shania, who immediately grabbed his finger and tugged at it playfully. Her laughter brought a warm smile to his face.

As he stood, Gino's expression turned thoughtful. "I can't help but worry about our money situation," he admitted.

Theresa gave a knowing smile. "Don't. It's December 30th, right?"

Gino nodded.

"Well," she explained, "when the Time Gates reset things for the new year, all the money we've spent won't have been spent at all."

"Because none of this was supposed to happen in the original version of 1995," Gino said, his smile returning as he caught on.

"Exactly," Theresa replied.

"She's been spending the same thirty thousand Euros over and over," Vandar added with a wry grin.

Gino raised an eyebrow. "And the account is still open?"

Theresa shrugged. "Technically, it never closes."

Vandar turned his focus back to the clearing. "We need to finish this," he said, his tone serious. "New Year's Eve is almost here."

Vandar moved the wheelbarrow closer to the trailer as Gino steadied it. Together, they maneuvered the final marble boulder into place. Vandar grunted with effort as he rolled it toward the last hollowed-out spot in the soil. He heaved the wheelbarrow handles upward, letting the rock slide down into its place with a dull thud. He sank onto the stone, wiping sweat from his brow, and surveyed the completed arrangement.

"You've done it," Theresa said, walking up beside him with Shania in her arms. Her voice carried a mix of pride and concern.

Vandar stood and began pointing to the stones, his excitement evident. "Horus," he said, gesturing to a large rock on the outer circle. "Earth, Saturn, Jupiter, the Sun," he continued, pointing to the central arrangement of smaller stones.

Gino followed his gestures, nodding thoughtfully. "Station

stones?" he asked, noticing the smaller rocks forming the perimeter.

"They represent the edges of the galaxy," Vandar explained. "The Milky Way."

Finally, Vandar knelt by a solitary stone set apart from the rest. He placed a hand on it, his expression heavy. "And this one... the Time Gates."

Gino frowned as he watched Vandar linger by the stone. "Will it work?" he asked, his voice low.

Vandar hesitated before answering. "I don't know," he admitted quietly.

"What happens if it doesn't?" Gino pressed. "To Theresa, to me?"

Vandar sighed deeply, standing to face him. "If it doesn't work, you'll vanish. You'll return to where you would have been in the world the Time Gates dictate for 1995."

Gino's face tightened. "And where is that?" he demanded.

Vandar looked away, unable to meet his gaze. "Anywhere. Perhaps you'd still be alive. Perhaps not."

The weight of his words hung in the air. Gino paced restlessly, his unease growing. "This is a gamble, Vandar—a huge one."

"I know," Vandar said, his voice tinged with frustration. "Do you think I haven't thought about this? I've gone over every possibility. This arrangement will shield us, just like Stonehenge. The ley lines here are strong enough to keep us safe."

Theresa stepped forward, her voice gentle but insistent. "Vandar, we need to consider the alternative."

"No," Vandar snapped, spinning to face her. "It will work."

"But if it doesn't?" she pressed, her eyes searching his. "What then?"

Vandar hesitated, his resolve wavering. "I'll find you," he said finally. "Even if you don't remember me, I'll find you."

Gino shook his head, his expression a mix of skepticism and sorrow. "And what will you do when we don't believe you? When we see you as a madman claiming to know us?"

Theresa's voice broke as tears welled in her eyes. "We can't even leave ourselves a message," she whispered. "The letters would disappear."

Vandar shut his eyes, his shoulders trembling. "It'll work," he said hoarsely. "It has to work."

Theresa walked to his side and embraced him as he wept. Gino sat down heavily on one of the stones, his thoughts consumed by everything they stood to lose. The year they'd spent together, the insights he'd gained about life and time—none of it would matter if the Time Gates erased it all. He would live out an ordinary life, ignorant of what had been stolen from him.

Vandar wiped his tears and looked at Gino and Theresa, his resolve hardening. "We can't risk going back to the ley line in England. The Carnos will be waiting for us. They expect us to return. Even if we survived, they could track us."

Gino nodded, understanding the risk.

Vandar knelt by the pram and looked into Shania's curious eyes. "My vision won't fail us. I promise you, I'll bring us all back here—together."

Theresa's gaze softened, her love for him shining through her tears. She placed a hand on his cheek. "We trust you," she said quietly.

Vandar leaned forward and kissed her, sealing his vow.

13

The two men sat on the tractor, watching the river's waters shimmer under the bright afternoon sun. The sky was a brilliant, cloudless blue, the kind that seemed endless in the Austrian summer. They had just finished the final touches on the stone arrangement and decided to rest before heading back to the farmhouse. Gino wiped his brow and glanced at Vandar, who was drinking deeply from a water bottle.

"So, who built the Time Gates?" Gino asked, his voice breaking the tranquil silence.

Vandar paused mid-drink, his expression contemplative. He studied Gino for a moment, as if weighing whether he was ready to hear the answer. Turning his gaze to the sparkling river, Vandar began, his voice low and measured.

"The Kaldros," he said. "He conquered all the free worlds and laid waste to his enemies. His army was unstoppable, moving at speeds no one else could match."

Vandar kicked a small stone at his feet, sending it tumbling toward the water's edge. "For five hundred years, he ruled the universe. He ordered the construction of the Time Gates at the cost of countless lives, obliterating planets and civilizations to achieve his vision. Even so, their existence was kept secret from the greater empire."

"Why keep it a secret?" Gino asked, frowning.

Vandar turned to him. "The Time Gates were the key to his

absolute control. If anyone learned of them—if they discovered how the Kaldrosdom's power worked—they would know how to bring it all down."

Gino stared at the young man beside him, the river reflecting flickers of sunlight on Vandar's serious face. This mysterious figure, who seemed to know so much about unimaginable things, suddenly felt more distant and enigmatic. Gino realized just how little he truly knew about him.

"Who are you, really?" Gino asked, his voice tinged with a mix of curiosity and unease.

Vandar took a breath and removed the metal bracelet he had often held in moments of reflection. He handed it to Gino. "I am the one who received the message from Tralonu ek Busca," he said, his tone calm but firm.

"Tralonu ek...?" Gino took the bracelet, inspecting it with newfound curiosity. It was a striking piece, its surface adorned with intricate symbols and strange, unfamiliar script. He ran his fingers over the patterns, marveling at its craftsmanship.

"That belonged to Tralonu," Vandar said, his gaze distant as if recalling a memory. "He wore it for many lonely years. He told me the Kaldrosdom must end. The balance of the galaxy must be restored."

Gino handed the bracelet back, his face a mixture of skepticism and wonder. "And he spoke to you? Personally?"

"Yes," Vandar replied with a faint smile, sensing Gino's doubt. "He gave me a mission."

Vandar's smile grew wider, and he let out a soft laugh. "Would you like to truly understand, Gino?"

"Yes," Gino said, his tone resolute. "I would."

"Then come with me," Vandar said, rising to his feet. "I'll show you what lies in the heavens."

Vandar led Gino to a flat, grassy patch near the riverbank. The sunlight gleamed on the water, and the rustling of leaves added a tranquil rhythm to the scene.

"Sit here," Vandar said, extending a hand to help Gino lower himself onto the dry soil. Gino accepted the gesture, settling in with a grunt.

Vandar sat cross-legged across from him, holding his hands out.

"Take my hands, and don't let go until we return."

Gino hesitated, then grasped Vandar's hands. "What exactly are we doing?"

"Trust me," Vandar said, his grip tightening. "Close your eyes."

Gino obeyed, though he couldn't ignore the heat of the sun on his face or the itch of the dry summer air. His restlessness grew as sweat trickled down his temple. But then, just as he was about to complain, a profound calmness washed over him. The warmth of the sun vanished. The sound of the river and the insects faded into silence.

When he opened his eyes, he gasped. They were no longer on Earth.

Gino found himself in a vast, black expanse—an infinite void. Small, dim stars began to flicker into existence around him, gradually growing brighter until the night sky was alive with light. He floated, weightless, surrounded by the majesty of the cosmos. The stars moved, their brilliance stretching into streaks of light as they traveled across his vision. Awe gripped him. He couldn't comprehend how he was here, suspended in the universe's endless expanse.

Somehow, he felt Vandar's presence, though he couldn't see him. Then Vandar's voice, steady and calm, resonated in his mind. "Get ready. We're going to move."

Before Gino could respond, they hurtled through space. A distant star grew rapidly, transforming from a speck into a massive burning sphere. Its fiery arms of heat reached toward them, radiating unimaginable energy. They lingered near it for a moment, Gino captivated by its terrifying beauty.

"That star is my point of reference," Vandar said. "It guides me to the beast."

"The beast?" Gino asked, his unease growing.

"Yes," Vandar replied. "You'll feel it soon."

As they moved again, faster than before, Gino felt a wave of dread creeping over him. A cold, oppressive emptiness weighed on his soul. "What is this feeling?" he asked, his voice trembling.

"You're sensing Horus."

Gino turned toward the source of the foreboding sensation—and froze.

In the distance, an incomprehensibly vast spiral loomed, its swirling colors pulling him into its gravitational grasp. At its center was an all-consuming black void—a black hole of unimaginable size. Even from this unfathomable distance, it dominated the heavens, devouring stars, planets, entire galaxies. Suns were crushed into nothingness, their light extinguished as they were consumed.

The sheer scale of its destruction overwhelmed Gino. He felt utterly insignificant, helpless against its insatiable hunger. His entire body trembled.

Gino woke with a jolt, gasping for air. The riverbank was back, the sound of flowing water and chirping birds grounding him. He ran a hand over his damp face, his heart racing.

Vandar sat calmly beside him, a knowing smile on his face. "So," he said softly, "are your eyes open now?"

Gino looked at him, pale and shaken. He nodded slowly, unable to speak.

Vandar chuckled, the sound both comforting and enigmatic. "Good."

Gino stared at him, the weight of what he had seen pressing heavily on his mind. For the first time, he truly believed Vandar—and it terrified him.

14

Vandar pushed open the farmhouse door, the cool air from outside following him in. His boots echoed softly against the wooden floor as he moved through the rooms.

"Theresa? Shania?" he called.

"Up here," came Theresa's voice from the bedroom.

He took the stairs two at a time, his heart pounding. When he reached the room, he found her cradling Shania in her arms, the child half-asleep, her small hand gripping the edge of her mother's blouse. Vandar sat on the edge of the bed, his presence tender yet heavy with exhaustion. He reached out to touch his daughter's cheek, her skin warm and soft beneath his fingers.

"It's finished," he said, his voice barely above a whisper. "The arrangement... it'll keep you and Shania here. With me."

Theresa's eyes glistened, and her lips trembled as she tried to speak. "Vandar," she began, her voice cracking.

"No," he interrupted gently, brushing away a tear as it slipped down her cheek. "Don't say it."

"If it doesn't work—"

"Stop," he pleaded, his own tears threatening to fall. "It will."

"If it doesn't," she continued firmly, her voice steadying despite her emotion, "you need to know that I accepted the risk. I chose this. Here, in Austria, or back in England, there was always a chance we wouldn't make it. But if we don't..." She paused, her gaze locking onto his. "It's not your fault. Promise me you'll keep going. You'll find a way."

He shook his head, overwhelmed. "Theresa, I can't—"

"You can," she said, gripping his hand tightly. "Because you must. For Shania. For the future."

Vandar pulled her into his arms, holding her as though sheer will alone could prevent anything from taking her away. "I love you," he whispered.

"I love you too," she replied, resting her head against his shoulder. "And no matter what happens, I always will."

15

New Year's Eve was unnaturally warm, the still air heavy with anticipation. The sun had sunk behind the jagged outline of the Alps, its final rays bleeding into the sky in shades of molten gold and deep crimson. By ten o'clock, the darkness had settled, broken only by the flickering light of a bonfire in the clearing.

They sat close to the flames, their shadows shifting across the arrangement of stones. Shania slept soundly in her pram, her soft breaths drowned out by the crackle of burning wood. It was a quiet gathering, each of them lost in their thoughts. As the hour crept closer to midnight, the tension grew palpable.

Vandar wrapped an arm around Theresa, holding her close. His hands were cold and clammy, and she could feel the tremble in his touch.

"It'll work," he murmured, more to himself than to her.

Theresa said nothing, only leaning into him.

Nearby, Gino pretended to be unaffected, sipping Chianti and nibbling on a piece of Panettone. But his jovial facade crumbled as the minutes ticked by, his glances at the sky growing more frequent. Finally, he set his glass aside and sighed heavily.

"Let's get to it," he said, standing.

Theresa rose and took her father's hand, guiding him to the center of the stone circle marked out with smaller rocks. Vandar followed, lifting Shania from her pram.

"My little girl," he whispered, cradling her close. He kissed her forehead, his tears glistening in the firelight. The weight of what he was about to do settled over him like a shroud. He memorized every detail of her face—her tiny nose, her soft curls, the peaceful expression that only a child could wear.

"I love you," he choked out, his voice breaking under the strain.

He walked slowly, each step feeling like a lifetime, until he reached Theresa and Gino.

"The time is upon us," Gino said quietly, his voice heavy with resignation.

Vandar handed Shania to Theresa and kissed her deeply. "I love you," she whispered.

He nodded, his smile weak but determined. Turning to Gino, he raised his hand in a small salute.

"Take care of them," Vandar said.

Gino returned the gesture, his eyes glistening.

Vandar stepped back, looking up at the sky. The darkness was softening, shifting to a deep blue as the stars burned brighter. A sudden gust of wind swept through the clearing, stirring the trees. He raised his arm, the symbols on his wristband glowing faintly in response.

"Let it work, Tralonu ek Busca," he prayed. "Let it carry them through."

Thunder cracked overhead, and the stars began to swirl. Their movements were no longer random but synchronized, as if part of some great celestial dance.

Vandar gasped. "He knows!"

The sky seemed to come alive, the Milky Way spinning like a tidal wave of light. Brilliant streaks of color arced across the heavens, illuminating the clearing.

"It's working!" Vandar shouted, his voice filled with relief.

Theresa tilted her head back, her face alight with awe. The winds grew stronger, whipping her hair around her face.

Then, from the shadows of the forest, a sudden flash of light erupted.

Gino cried out as the impact struck him square in the chest, his body flung several meters from the circle. Theresa screamed, dropping to her knees beside him.

Vandar turned toward the source of the attack, his stomach sinking. Emerging from the treeline was a woman with fiery red hair, dressed in the black uniform of the Kaldrosdom's elite. She holstered her pistol and broke into a sprint, moving with lethal precision.

"Memphys," Vandar whispered, his voice thick with disbelief.

The woman vaulted over one of the outer stones, her movements fluid and controlled. Vandar snapped out of his daze and bolted toward Theresa, desperate to intercept her before it was too late.

Theresa crouched over Gino, her heart hammering. "Dad?" she called, shaking his shoulder. He didn't respond. Smoke rose from the charred wound in his side, and his breathing was faint, if there at all.

Shania stirred in her arms, wide-eyed and frightened. Theresa held her closer, willing herself to stay calm.

The sound of approaching footsteps made her turn. Memphys was closing in, her expression cold and determined. Theresa's instincts screamed danger. She clutched Shania tightly and tried to run, but Memphys was too fast.

The red-haired woman lunged, but a heavy impact sent her sprawling. Vandar tackled her to the ground, pinning her briefly before she freed herself with a flurry of blows. Both combatants scrambled to their feet, their eyes locking in a deadly standoff.

"Vandar Manak," Memphys sneered, blood trickling from the corner of her mouth.

"Your fight is with me," Vandar said, his tone ice cold. "Leave them out of this."

Memphys smirked. "Oh, Vandar. You really thought you could escape the Time Gates? Ilores told me everything."

Vandar's stomach turned. "You're making a mistake."

Memphys circled him like a predator, her pistol raised. Vandar risked a glance at his watch—forty-five seconds to midnight.

"Theresa!" he shouted. "Take Shania to the center! Now!"

Theresa hesitated, her heart breaking as she looked at Gino. But she knew Vandar was right. She backed toward the center of the stones, her steps unsteady.

Vandar's voice snapped her focus back. "In the circle—and don't move!"

Memphys lunged, but Vandar was faster, knocking her pistol from her hand with a swift kick. The weapon skittered across the clearing, disappearing among the stones. Memphys growled in frustration and unleashed a barrage of kicks, each one landing with brutal precision. Vandar staggered, dazed, and Memphys pounced.

She wrapped a cord around his neck, pulling it tight. Vandar gasped, clawing at the cord as his vision darkened.

Theresa watched in horror, torn between helping him and staying in the circle. Her eyes darted to the sky—midnight was seconds away. She grabbed an empty Chianti bottle and hurled it with all her strength.

The bottle struck Memphys' head with a resounding crack. She stumbled, releasing Vandar, who collapsed to the ground, gasping for air.

Memphys staggered to her feet, blood dripping from her temple. She retrieved her pistol and aimed it at Theresa.

"You're done," she snarled.

Vandar forced himself to stand, his vision blurred and his body weak.

"Stay in the circle, Theresa," he croaked.

His watch beeped—midnight.

Memphys squeezed the trigger, but before the shot could land, Theresa and Shania were consumed by a radiant burst of light. The energy engulfed them, blinding Memphys. Her shot went wide, hitting one of the stones.

When the light faded, Theresa and Shania were gone.

Vandar staggered forward, his fist colliding with Memphys' jaw. She crumpled to the ground, unconscious.

The clearing was silent. Vandar fell to his knees, tears streaming down his face. They were gone.

But then he heard it—a soft, familiar chuckle.

He turned toward the stones, his breath catching. Shania sat there, unharmed, her tiny laugh cutting through the silence.

Vandar scooped her into his arms, holding her tightly. "You're still here," he whispered. "You're still here."

As the first light of dawn broke over the Alps, Vandar drove south into Italy, leaving the clearing—and Memphys—behind. He had lost so much, but as he glanced at Shania in the rearview mirror, he knew he still had hope.

16

The years passed, and before Vandar realized it, Shania was a teenager. She had grown into a sharp, independent young woman, her curiosity and determination a constant source of pride—and occasional challenge.

But now, as she edged closer to adulthood, she was beginning to wrestle with questions that Vandar had known would come. Questions he wasn't sure he could answer. For the first time, her differences from others began to matter.

And the reason was Richard.

Richard Brooks lived down the road, a typical English lad with a cheeky grin and a love for cars and football. But he was also kind, polite, and—Vandar had to admit—charmingly earnest. He spent every spare moment with Shania, and Vandar didn't mind. Richard wasn't a yob like some of the other neighborhood boys, and he had a good head on his shoulders.

Still, Vandar couldn't help but notice the way Shania had been preoccupied lately, her usual confidence giving way to moments of quiet doubt. One evening, the tension finally surfaced.

"September, October, November, and December…"

Vandar glanced up from the sink, his hands submerged in soapy water, and raised an eyebrow at Shania's odd remark. She stood leaning against the fridge, arms folded tightly across her chest.

"You've got it right, if that's what you're asking," he said with a small smile, turning back to the dishes.

She sighed, her fingers drumming against her arm.

Vandar wiped a plate and set it aside. "Out with it," he said, his tone light but probing.

"What?" she replied, her voice strained with an edge of defensiveness.

"What's bothering you?" he asked, turning to face her fully.

For a moment, she hesitated, staring at the floor as though searching for the right words. Finally, she spoke, her voice soft but weighted with unspoken fears.

"When January comes, he won't remember me, will he?"

Vandar's hands stilled. He turned back to her, drying his hands with a tea towel, and met her gaze.

"Who?" he asked, though he already suspected the answer.

She bit her lip, refusing to look at him.

"Oh," he said, understanding dawning. "Richard."

She nodded, her shoulders sagging as she let out a shaky breath.

Vandar studied her carefully. She wasn't his little girl anymore; her growing confidence and independence were evident. And yet, in this moment, she seemed as vulnerable as the child who had clung to him in the aftermath of the Alps.

"It's something we can't control," he said quietly.

"But I like him, Dad," she said, her voice breaking with frustration.

Vandar sighed, his heart heavy. "I know, honey. But we're different."

Her head snapped up, her eyes brimming with tears. "Why are we different?" she demanded. "I don't want to be this way!"

Vandar stepped forward and wrapped his arms around her, holding her tightly as she cried into his chest. He could feel the years of questions, doubt, and frustration pouring out of her in those tears.

For a long moment, the kitchen was silent, save for the hum of the fridge and the occasional drip from the faucet.

Finally, Shania pulled back, brushing her tears away with trembling fingers. Her voice steadied, though her eyes still glistened.

"Really, Dad," she said, her tone more resolute. "I've always just accepted it before. But I can't anymore. I need to know. Why am I like this? Why us?"

Vandar sighed, gesturing for her to sit at the kitchen table. He followed, pulling out a chair across from her. For a moment, he sat in silence, studying her face. She had Theresa's determination and warmth, and the thought of disappointing her cut deeper than he cared to admit.

"You're going to hear some things you won't like," he said finally, his voice low and serious.

"I'm ready," she replied, meeting his gaze without wavering.

Vandar nodded, his heart aching. He had dreaded this conversation for years, knowing it would bring more questions than answers. But he owed her the truth—or at least as much of it as he understood.

17

PART II

THE TRIALS OF VANDAR

After bringing the planet Ethsiz to its knees, Commander Vandar Manak returned with his unit to the Mothership. Victory was predictable, yet the crew celebrated with the fervor of true believers. Drinks, laughter, and games filled the corridors, their voices rising in a chorus of devotion: "Long live the Kaldros—grant him a thousand more years!"

The Mothership cut through the void of space, its next destination looming on the horizon: Jupiter. Rebellion awaited, but for now, the soldiers were granted 145 Earth hours of rest. A brief reprieve, though never truly restful; the shadow of war always lingered.

Vandar joined the celebrations for a time, raising a glass to the Kaldros alongside his comrades. Yet, as the night wore on, he felt the weight of exhaustion creeping in. His body ached, his muscles heavy from battle. Victory may have been sweet, but the toll was undeniable.

Eventually, he retreated to his quarters. The sterile silence of the small room felt like a balm. He climbed into his bunk, letting his eyes close as exhaustion pulled him into its depths.

The sleep came easily, deep and heavy. But just as easily, it was broken.

Vandar stirred, rolling onto his side in search of comfort. That's when he heard it—a faint wheeze, deep in his throat.

He froze, listening carefully. The sound was barely perceptible, almost buried beneath the steady thrum of his pulse. For a moment, he thought it was gone, but then he realized: the wheeze wasn't tied to his breathing. It was in sync with his heartbeat.

Unease prickled at the edges of his thoughts. He pressed two fingers to his throat, feeling his pulse. The sound was there, faint but rhythmic, perfectly aligned with the beat of his heart.

Vandar swung his legs over the side of the bunk and made his way to the small bathroom adjoining his quarters. The fluorescent light flickered slightly as he leaned over the sink, staring into the mirror. His face looked normal—calm, even.

But the sound persisted.

He pressed his fingers along his throat, searching for a lump or irregularity, but felt nothing out of the ordinary. Still, the noise was there, a crackling rhythm that refused to leave his mind.

Opening the medkit mounted on the wall, he retrieved a pair of medical tongs. For a moment, he hesitated, staring at the cold, gleaming metal in his hand. Then, gritting his teeth, he opened his mouth and carefully inserted the tongs.

The sensation was uncomfortable, but he pushed deeper, probing until he felt resistance.

Something solid.

His breath hitched. It wasn't a part of him.

Vandar opened the tongs slightly, gripping the object, and withdrew them. He gagged and coughed, mucus splattering into the sink. When he finally looked at the end of the tongs, his stomach twisted.

A tiny parasite wriggled in their grasp.

Its back was hard, like a glossy black shell, while its underside was pale and soft. Its bloated belly, filled with dark red blood, pulsed faintly. Vandar stared, horrified, as he realized it had been feeding on him. Two small black eyes sat on its grotesque face, unseeing yet somehow menacing.

It writhed, its barbed legs rasping together, scraping against the tongs as it squirmed. Vandar's breath quickened. It felt as if the creature was watching him, planning its way back inside.

Disgust surged through him, and he flung it into the corner of the bathroom. Without hesitation, he crushed it under his boot, the crunch of its shell shattering echoing in the small space.

He leaned over the sink, gagging, bile rising in his throat. But he stopped short of vomiting. His mind raced, questions tumbling over each other.

What was that thing? How did it get there? Has it been inside me for days? Weeks?

The thought of its barbed legs lodged in his throat, its belly swelling with his blood, made him shudder. He rinsed his mouth, trying to steady his breathing. After a long moment, he decided: no one could know about this. The medics were ruthless, and any weakness would mark him as expendable.

Over the next few days, Vandar did his best to act normal. Though he ran a fever and felt drained, he refused to visit the medics. Instead, he pushed through the discomfort, waiting for his body to recover.

When his strength returned, he noticed something… different.

At first, he thought it was his imagination, a trick of the mind. But it persisted. He felt sharper, more reflective. His thoughts, once laser-focused on obedience and duty, began to stray.

He started noticing things he hadn't before: the clumsiness of his comrades, their blind adherence to orders. They were efficient, yes, but they were also unthinking, reliant on brute force to solve problems. Their simplicity irritated him in a way it never had before.

Why now? he wondered. Was it the parasite? Had it somehow dulled my mind, and now, without it, I'm seeing clearly? Or has something changed in me because of it?

18

The Mothership entered Jupiter's orbit, its shadow cutting through the swirling storm clouds below. The gas giant's atmosphere raged in shades of orange and red, its hurricane-force winds an unending chaos. Small offensive ships descended from the Mothership, plunging into the tempest toward their objective: the captured entrances to the miners' labyrinthine tunnels.

Vandar Manak stood in the landing bay as his ship touched down. The cavernous chamber vibrated faintly, the distant roar of Jupiter's storms reverberating through the walls. Soldiers shouted orders over the noise of unloading equipment, their movements efficient and practiced. Vandar watched his unit with the eye of a commander, ensuring everything was in order.

"You're lucky to have made it down here alive," the Marshall said, appearing beside him.

Vandar turned to the man, his expression neutral.

"I personally believe Jupiter's atmosphere to be the worst to land through in the entire solar system—at least among the outer planets," the Marshall continued, his tone half-joking but edged with truth.

Vandar shrugged, his focus still on the troopers. "What are our orders?"

The Marshall's grin faded, replaced by a more serious expression. "The rebels are fighting a strong defense. This won't be a quick operation." He gestured to a group of soldiers inspecting drilling equipment. "The tunnel system is a nightmare. It's impossible to fully secure a sector without overwhelming manpower. The miners know the terrain better than we ever could, and they've rigged traps everywhere."

Vandar nodded, already considering the tactical implications. "Why have the miners turned on the Kaldros?"

The Marshall hesitated, glancing around before lowering his voice. "It's believed they're stalling for time, trying to arrange transport off the planet—to the Genowan System."

Vandar raised an eyebrow. "Transport for what?"

The Marshall avoided his gaze. "That's above my pay grade," he said curtly.

Vandar frowned but didn't press further. Instead, he shifted his thoughts to the rebels' position. "They can't win. The air supply—"

"Has been terminated," the Marshall interrupted. "In six days, the atmosphere in the tunnels will no longer be breathable. Resistance won't last a week."

Vandar's tactical mind churned. The situation seemed straightforward: cut off from breathable air, the rebels' defeat was inevitable. Yet, the Kaldros's orders to act now suggested something urgent, something worth risking lives to obtain.

"What could be so vital that the Kaldros won't simply wait them out?" Vandar wondered aloud.

The Marshall stopped walking and turned to him, his expression calculated. "Orders came directly from Ilores and the Kaldros. Even the Carnos are being sent in. Whatever the miners are hiding, it's important."

Vandar stiffened slightly at the mention of the Carnos—the Kaldros's elite warriors, feared even among the highest ranks.

The Marshall's tone shifted, becoming almost conspiratorial. "I've found a way into the heart of the rebel compound," he said. "An old construction tunnel, left from the days when this city was being built. It could take you and a select group of soldiers directly into the center of their operations. You could capture whatever it is they're protecting—and bring glory to the Kaldros."

Vandar felt a flicker of instinctive pride at the words. Glory for the Kaldros, honor for his unit—it was what he had been trained to desire. But beneath the surface, a shadow of doubt crept in.

"You have a reputation, Vandar Manak," the Marshall continued, his tone smooth and persuasive. "Your unit boasts high success and low mortality rates. Complete this mission, and you could be on the path to joining the Carnos themselves."

Vandar's chest tightened. The offer should have filled him with pride, but instead, it felt hollow. The doubts he had buried since the incident on the Mothership stirred once more.

Why should I risk myself for the Kaldros's glory?

The thought was treasonous, unthinkable. Yet, it refused to leave his mind. For the first time in his career, Vandar felt the weight of uncertainty pressing against the doctrines he had once held sacred.

He glanced at the Marshall, whose grin had faded into a faint frown of suspicion. Vandar realized he had been silent too long.

"For the glory of the Kaldros!" Vandar declared sharply, raising a salute.

The Marshall's grin returned. "Excellent. Ready your men. I'll brief you in twenty minutes."

Vandar nodded, watching as the Marshall walked away, his polished boots clicking against the stone floor.

When the man was gone, Vandar exhaled slowly, the tension in his chest refusing to dissipate.

What's happening to me? he thought. Am I losing my faith?

He turned to watch his unit as they prepared for the mission. They moved with disciplined efficiency, their faces alight with determination and excitement. They believed in the Kaldros, in the righteousness of their cause. They trusted him to lead them. Vandar clenched his fists, trying to banish the whispers in his mind.

It will fade once I'm back in battle, he told himself. This is where I belong.

But as he prepared for the mission, the doubts remained, nagging at the edges of his thoughts. They were questions he couldn't yet answer—questions that would not stay buried.

19

The tunnel was pitch black, unbearably hot, and barely wide enough to crawl through. Vandar had chosen a dozen of his most skilled troopers for the mission, and now, after nearly an hour of crawling through the stifling pipe, they were drenched in sweat and gasping for air.

Vandar, leading the way, reached the grate at the tunnel's end. The cool air beyond was a relief, and he silently thanked his position at the front as he retrieved his pocket torch. The hum of the tool echoed sharply in the oppressive silence as he worked to cut through the metal.

After a few minutes, the grate gave way, and Vandar wrenched it free. When he turned to check on his team, the count was ten—two men had collapsed from oxygen deprivation before reaching the exit.

He glanced at the schematic display on his wrist. "Intelligence suggests these accommodation units are housing the leaders of the resistance," he said, pointing to a multi-level structure on the map.

"Simple plan: mutual offensive and backup. Sweep the building from bottom to top. Kill all targets."

The troopers nodded grimly.

"Let's move," Vandar ordered.

The resistance was ill-prepared and disorganized, their defenses crumbling under the troopers' assault.

The most difficult part of the mission was breaching the building's entrance. An explosive trap on the walkway claimed two more soldiers, while the rest narrowly escaped plummeting into the chasm below. Heavy fire from above forced them to scale the walls, but their climbing skills proved invaluable, and they secured the first floor with ruthless efficiency.

As they advanced through the building, Vandar caught sight of a transport ship on the roof. High above the skyscrapers, at the pinnacle of the dome, he saw safety doors marked with warning signs.

"Those doors open directly to the surface," he muttered.

It was clear the rebels were working to bypass the safety protocols that prevented the airlock's activation. If they succeeded, they could escape into Jupiter's stormy atmosphere. Time was critical.

Vandar split his team into pairs, ordering them to secure the roof by any means necessary. Tharon, his communications officer, stayed at his side. Together, they swept through the floors with blaster fire and small explosives, dismantling improvised obstacles.

The miners they encountered were poorly trained and disorganized, their resistance easily crushed. But Tharon began to notice something troubling.

Vandar wasn't taking his usual kill shots. His aim, once unforgivingly precise, now seemed restrained. Instead of lethal strikes, he fired to disable, leaving targets alive where possible.

The turning point came when they encountered an older miner—a pot-bellied, slow-moving man who charged toward them with desperate, erratic shots.

The man's fire was wild but dangerously close. Vandar, the nearer of the two, raised his weapon, aiming for the miner's shoulder. But he hesitated.

"Commander!" Tharon shouted, panic edging his voice.

Tharon raised his blaster and fired, a clean shot between the miner's eyes. The man crumpled to the ground, lifeless.

"What's happened to you?" Tharon demanded, his voice low and accusatory.

Vandar frowned, his jaw tightening. "I'm fine," he said curtly.

"Bullshit!" Tharon spat, glaring at him.

Vandar met his gaze with icy resolve. "Let's keep moving."

* * *

Suddenly, a massive explosion rocked the building, the shockwave knocking them both to the ground.

"What the hell was that?" Tharon yelled, clutching his head as the deafening sound reverberated in his ears.

Vandar staggered to his feet and moved to a nearby window. Smoke and flames engulfed the roof, the skeletal remains of the transport ship visible through the haze.

"The transport," he said grimly. "It's been destroyed."

Tharon joined him, a smug grin spreading across his face. "One of us must've made it and taken care of it."

Vandar spoke into his helmet's microphone. "Come in, all units. Status report—repeat: status report."

A crackle of static preceded the reply. "This is Alpha. Enemy transport destroyed. Pursuing fugitives on the west side of the building."

Vandar checked his schematic. "They're heading toward the private apartment complex," he said.

"They're trapped," Tharon said with a grin, loading his blaster. "Let's finish this."

They rounded a corner and spotted the fugitives—a man and woman sprinting for the apartment doorway, a small girl clutched in the man's arms.

Vandar's breath caught. These weren't miners or soldiers—they were civilians.

Tharon opened fire, shattering the door's glass panels in a hail of bullets. The family dove to the ground, shielding themselves as shards of glass rained down.

"Tharon!" Vandar shouted, shoving the blaster down. "Stand down!"

"What the hell are you talking about?" Tharon snapped. "They're traitors!"

"And they're unarmed," Vandar countered. "I want them interrogated."

Tharon sneered but lowered his weapon. "Since when?"

Vandar ignored him and pushed through the broken door.

* * *

Inside the apartment, the family huddled against the wall. The woman sobbed, her bruised face streaked with tears. The child's wide eyes were fixed on Vandar, her body trembling. The man stepped forward, his expression resolute despite his fear.

"My name is Arapeta," he said. "Take my life for the Kaldros, but spare the woman and child. I alone am the traitor."

Tharon spat on the floor. "You're not in a position to make demands."

Vandar silenced him with a sharp gesture. He studied Arapeta, noting the man's composure and his attire, which marked him as someone of rank.

"What is the reason for your betrayal?" Vandar asked. "Why resist the Kaldros?"

Arapeta met his gaze. "The Kaldros is no savior," he said. "He's a tyrant who bends the laws of nature to his will. He's not just ruling us —he's twisting the very fabric of time itself. And it will destroy us all."

Vandar stared at him, stunned. Then he noticed the silver bracelet on Arapeta's wrist, its design unlike anything he'd seen.

"I had to try," Arapeta continued. "The free world must know. They are our last hope."

"You've failed," Vandar said quietly, his tone reflective.

"To try was all we could do," Arapeta replied. "The truth must outlive us."

Before Vandar could respond, the room lit up with blaster fire.

Tharon fired without warning, the shot hitting Arapeta squarely in the chest. The man collapsed, blood pooling beneath him.

"Bastard!" Vandar roared, striking Tharon with the butt of his weapon. The blow sent him sprawling, his blaster firing wildly.

Vandar turned just in time to see the woman and child collapse, their bodies riddled with stray shots.

Vandar froze, his breath caught in his throat.

"What have you done?" he whispered.

Tharon, dazed, tried to raise his weapon again, but Vandar fired first.

Tharon crumpled to the floor, lifeless, a pool of blood spreading around him.

Vandar stood there, his blaster still raised. Around him lay the bodies of the family and his soldier. The silence pressed in, suffocating.

What am I becoming?

20

Vandar stood frozen, as still as a statue. Time seemed to stop, the world narrowing to the carnage around him. He stared at Tharon's lifeless body, the weight of what he had done pressing down on him like a crushing tide.

Had he really just killed another Kaldrosdom officer?

His eyes drifted toward the fugitives. They, too, lay motionless. He stumbled backward, his weapon slipping from his hand with a clatter. Slowly, he approached the bodies, his breathing shallow and ragged.

The man's head was unrecognizable, shattered by Tharon's blaster. The little girl lay limp, her eyes wide but lifeless. Vandar's knees buckled, and he collapsed in front of her. For the first time in his life as a soldier, he cried.

He reached out and touched the girl's tiny hand. It was still warm. He cradled it in his own and whimpered, his tears soaking into the cold floor.

Then, a faint groan broke through the silence.

Vandar's head snapped up. The sound had come from the woman, slumped against the wall. He rushed to her side. Blood seeped from her abdomen, staining her clothes. She looked up at him, her eyes desperate but strangely calm.

"I... I'm sorry," Vandar said, the words spilling out of him. He repeated them again and again. They were all he had.

The woman stared at him, her expression softening despite the pain. "Please..." she whispered, her voice trembling.

He leaned closer. "What do you need? Tell me."

Her lips quivered. "You are... the only chance... to stop the Kaldros."

Vandar's brow furrowed. "Stop the Kaldros?" he spluttered, the idea absurd and unimaginable.

"You must," she said, her words coming slower now, her strength fading.

Desperate to help her, Vandar dug into his first aid kit. He pulled out a small glass vial, snapped it open, and handed it to her. "Drink this," he urged.

She took it, her hand trembling. He sprayed an aerosol over her wound, the medical sealant stinging as it made contact.

"This will stop the bleeding," he said, though he knew it was a lie. She smiled faintly, seeing through him.

"I'm going to die," she said softly. "I've known that since the day I chose to oppose the Kaldros."

Vandar stared at her, struck by her quiet conviction.

"You're not like them," she continued, her voice weakening.

He shook his head. "You're wrong. I'm just as bad as all of them."

"No," she whispered, touching his arm. "You didn't know before. Now, you have a choice."

The sound of heavy footsteps echoed from the hallway, growing louder. Vandar's head snapped toward the door.

"They're coming," he muttered, his heart racing.

He jumped to his feet and ran to the door, slamming it shut and locking it. A heavy shelf nearby caught his eye, and he dragged it across the door to barricade it.

The banging started moments later, loud and insistent. The troopers wouldn't wait long before using explosives to breach the door.

"We have to move," Vandar said, glancing around the apartment.

"Wait," the woman rasped. She gestured toward her husband's body. "The bracelet... take it."

Vandar hurried to the man's body, unfastening the silver bracelet from his wrist. Meanwhile, the woman rummaged through her pockets, pulling out a small metal case. Relief flickered across her face when she found it.

Vandar glanced nervously at the barricaded door as the pounding grew more violent. "It won't fit in my pocket," he muttered, holding the bracelet.

"Put it on," she said firmly.

Without arguing, Vandar slipped the bracelet onto his wrist and scooped her up. He carried her to the far side of the room, opening a door that led to an outdoor balcony.

The air outside was smoky and thin, difficult to breathe. He set her down gently and ran back to secure the door.

"There's a lock button—red," she said weakly.

Vandar pressed it, and the door slammed shut.

"They'll be through eventually," he said, glancing nervously at the nearby windows overlooking the balcony.

"Never mind that," she replied.

Vandar returned to her side, her breathing shallow. She retrieved the metal case and opened it, revealing a tiny blade and a small circuit encased in clear resin.

"They'll leave me to die," she said. "But they'll take you... for the Kaldros's Military Police."

Vandar's stomach twisted. He knew what that meant.

The woman took his arm and pressed the blade against his skin. "Hold still," she said.

"What are you—" Vandar began, but stopped as she looked into his eyes.

"Trust me," she said.

The blade cut into his arm, sharp and deliberate. Blood welled up as she worked quickly, clearing the area with her shirt. The door rattled again, followed by muffled blaster fire.

Vandar flinched but didn't resist. He owed her this.

The woman inserted the circuit beneath his skin, her hands shaking from exhaustion. "Almost done," she whispered, pulling out a curved needle and thread.

Her face was pale now, her lips tinged with blue. She handed him the thread. "Sew yourself shut," she said weakly.

Vandar obeyed, his hands trembling as he worked. The process was surreal, the pain distant beneath the adrenaline coursing through him. The woman held the skin taut, guiding him despite her fading strength.

When the task was done, she collapsed onto the cold concrete, her eyes heavy.

"What's your name?" Vandar asked, his voice cracking.

She smiled faintly. "Aurora," she said.

Her gaze shifted to the bracelet on his wrist. "Hide it under your uniform," she murmured. "Don't take it off. Don't let them find it."

"But why?" Vandar asked. "And the circuit—what does it do?"

Aurora's breaths were shallow now, but she pressed on. "It's… the key. To the Kaldros's defenses… the Time Gates."

"The Time Gates?" Vandar echoed, his heart pounding.

She nodded faintly. "Everything else… Traluno ek Busca will guide you."

"Who?" Vandar asked desperately, leaning closer.

But Aurora's eyes fluttered shut. Her body went still in his arms.

"Aurora?" he called, shaking her gently. "Aurora!"

But she was gone.

21

Vandar gently laid Aurora's body in the small garden on the balcony, beneath the oppressive metal dome that loomed overhead. The sky within the dome was lifeless, a cold imitation of the real thing. He knelt beside her, staring at her still form, guilt churning in his chest. He had promised himself to protect her, but now all he could do was leave her here. Alone.

Soon, the invading forces would tear this place apart, filling the air with smoke and death. Her body would become part of the ruins — a silent warning to the rest of the universe. Vandar clenched his fists, his grief and frustration clawing at his insides. How many more will I fail before this ends?

As he rose to his feet, a wave of dizziness hit him, and he staggered, gripping a nearby pillar for support.

The air, he realized. It was thin and barely breathable.

Frantically, he checked his backpack for his re-breather. It wasn't there. Somewhere in the chaos, it must have been lost. His breathing grew ragged as his vision blurred, the world tilting around him. He needed to find air — and fast.

The sharp sound of boots landing on concrete jolted him. Vandar turned to see Tomo Labrak standing on the balcony.

Tomo's blaster was aimed at Vandar, his stance confident and ready. Most notably, he was wearing a re-breather.

Vandar staggered toward him, his steps unsteady. His mind swirled with a single thought: Take the re-breather.

Tomo smirked, tossing his blaster aside. "Come on, Commander," he taunted, dropping into a low fighting stance.

Vandar swung clumsily, his fists slow and unfocused. Tomo sidestepped easily, delivering a sharp blow to Vandar's ribs. The impact sent a jolt of pain through Vandar's chest, but he lunged again, desperation overriding reason.

Tomo struck again, this time landing a brutal punch to Vandar's jaw. Stars burst in Vandar's vision as he crumpled to the ground, Tomo's laughter echoing in his ears before everything went dark.

Vandar drifted in and out of consciousness, the world around him a distorted blur. Voices reached him, muffled and distant.

"I say kill him now!" Tomo's angry voice broke through the fog.

"You want to be court-martialed, you idiot?" another voice snapped. "Tie him up. The Marshall will decide his fate."

Vandar felt the rough scrape of ropes binding his arms and legs.

"Give him some air, or he'll die before we even get him there," the second voice added grudgingly.

The sensation of a re-breather being strapped to his face brought a fleeting moment of relief.

"But keep him out," the voice continued.

A sharp crack followed, and Vandar's world exploded in red as Tomo's fist connected with his face. Darkness swallowed him once more.

When Vandar awoke, it could have been hours—or days. He had no way of knowing.

He was breathing through a tube, his body tightly encased in thick fabric. His arms and legs were immobile, bound as if he were a mummy awaiting burial. He struggled to move, but the restraints held firm.

Above him, a blinding light seared his eyes. He squinted, trying to make sense of his surroundings. A shadow leaned over him, blocking the light for a moment. He blinked, his vision slowly adjusting, and the shadow resolved into a face.

The Marshall.

"Vandar Manak," the Marshall intoned, his voice devoid of emotion. "For treason against the Kaldros, the murder of a soldier of the Kaldrosdom, and the assault of a Kaldrosdom officer, you are hereby sentenced to face judgment at the Kaldros's Royal Prison."

Vandar's heart sank as the stretcher was lifted and tilted upright. His limbs were useless, his mind groggy and slow.

The Marshall stepped aside, and a massive machine rolled into view—a Narco-capsule. Vandar recognized it immediately: a freezing unit designed to place prisoners in stasis for long space journeys.

"May the Kaldros be merciful," the Marshall said with mock reverence.

Two soldiers unfastened the straps holding Vandar to the stretcher. They lifted him by the fabric cocoon and placed him inside the capsule.

Vandar's eyes darted around wildly, searching for a way out, but his body refused to cooperate.

The glass door of the capsule slid shut with a hiss, sealing him inside. The Marshall's face hovered just beyond the glass, a cruel smile curling his lips.

Vandar's breath came in short gasps as the walls of the capsule erupted with liquid nitrogen. The freezing mist surged around him, sharp and relentless.

It felt like his skin was being pierced by a thousand icy needles. His muscles spasmed involuntarily as the temperature plummeted. His lungs burned, each breath more painful than the last.

Through the frost and his own fading consciousness, Vandar could just make out the Marshall's expression, twisted in satisfaction.

Then, with one final, searing jolt, the world vanished, and Vandar was frozen solid.

22

The starship tumbled through the void of space, its sleek, reflective edges vanishing into the surrounding darkness. It moved with calculated precision, corkscrewing toward its destination—a maximum-security prison on Venus. The mission was simple: transport its frozen cargo of prisoners from Jupiter.

On the bridge, First Officer Yotra Peak sat at the controls, his sharp blue eyes scanning the screens ahead of him. The console lights pulsed softly, bathing the sterile bridge in cool hues of blue and green. The faint hum of the engines vibrated through the floor, a constant reminder of the vast emptiness pressing against the ship's hull. As both pilot and Narcologist, Yotra had dual responsibilities: navigating the ship and maintaining the cryogenic systems that kept the prisoners locked in stasis.

"Post-launch status, Minx," he said, his tone calm but commanding.

"The ship's status is stable," the ship's computer replied in its robotic female voice.

The bridge doors slid open with a soft hiss, and Second Officer Memphys Crowley strode in. She moved with confidence, her tall frame and bright orange curls catching the sterile light. Sliding into the co-pilot's seat, she adjusted the controls with quick, efficient movements.

"The load doors are intact. Everything alright up here, Sir?" she asked crisply.

Yotra raised an eyebrow. "You can call me Yotra," he replied.

"First names are not standard on any Kaldrosdom starship, Sir," she said stiffly.

"Well then, Officer Crowley," Yotra said with a wry smile, "the First Officer has ensured all prisoners are in proper cryogenic sleep. Everything is as it should be."

This was their second voyage together, and the atmosphere between them remained cold. Prisoner transport missions were crewed by only two people, which meant long hours in close quarters with someone you might not like. Yotra had no personal grudge against Crowley, but her blind devotion to the Kaldrosdom grated on him. She was a textbook Kaldrosdom officer: disciplined, self-righteous, and fanatically loyal to the Kaldros.

Yotra, on the other hand, had no such illusions. He was a skilled pilot, recruited not for loyalty but necessity. The Kaldrosdom needed people like him to keep its empire running, and he needed their money to navigate its labyrinthine bureaucracy. It was a fragile arrangement, one false move away from accusations of treason—or worse.

Memphys, though young at twenty-four, seemed oblivious to such risks. She had risen from her humble Earth roots to a position of authority, and it had clearly gone to her head. Yotra noted her polished uniform and the way she held herself with exaggerated pride. She had the zeal of someone who hadn't yet seen the darker side of the Kaldrosdom's rule.

As she reviewed the life-support systems for the prisoners, Memphys muttered, "Traitorous bastards. Any trouble with them, and our orders are to dump them into deep space."

"I'm aware of the protocol, Crowley," Yotra said flatly.

Memphys glanced at him, her expression smug. "How is it you outrank me?" she asked, her tone dripping with disdain. "You're not even a proper Kaldrosdom officer."

"Because without me, this ship wouldn't fly," Yotra replied with a humorless grin.

She snorted. "Hah. Why don't you just go to Saturn and take the oath to the Kaldros's rule? Then maybe you'll be worth that rank."

Yotra studied her carefully, his expression unreadable. "Because people are never the same when they return," he said quietly.

Memphys smirked, leaning back in her chair. "Whatever," she said dismissively, though her voice wavered for just a moment. "I've been to Saturn myself, and I've never been better."

Yotra's gaze lingered on her as she turned back to her console, her words ringing in his ears. There was something unnerving about the way people spoke after taking the oath, their enthusiasm hollow and rehearsed. He'd seen it before—bright-eyed recruits returning from Saturn with something missing. Their eyes seemed duller, their smiles strained. Whatever happened on Saturn, it changed them.

"Of course," he murmured under his breath, "you'd think that."

23

The bishop slid across the holographic chessboard, threatening two of Yotra's pieces.

"It's your move," Minx said, her robotic voice cool and neutral.

Yotra leaned forward, studying the game intently. He moved his rook with a flick of his finger, confident in his strategy.

"You're in check," Minx announced.

"What?" Yotra frowned, scanning the board. "No, I'm not."

Minx didn't respond.

"Minx, I'm not in check," he repeated, his voice edged with irritation.

Silence.

"Minx?!"

This time, only a faint buzzing came from the speakers. Yotra turned to the nearest screen, his frustration mounting.

"What the fuck now?" he muttered, initiating a system diagnostic.

Lines of code scrolled across the display, but they revealed nothing conclusive.

"What's wrong with you now, you stupid—"

Memphys Crowley delivered a sharp combination of blows in the gymnasium. A dominant-hand punch flowed into a left jab, followed by a precise roundhouse kick. She finished with a flourish, drawing her laser pistol in one smooth motion.

"Not bad," she said to herself, wiping sweat from her brow. Her orange curls stuck to her forehead, but she barely noticed, focused on refining her moves.

"Officer Crowley?" Minx's voice crackled through the gym's speakers.

"Yes, Minx?" Memphys replied, stretching her arms.

"There's a problem with the prisoners' area—chamber five."

Memphys groaned. "What kind of problem?"

"Nothing major," Minx said. "It seems to be a minor configuration difficulty."

Memphys rolled her eyes as she walked toward the gym's door. "Tell Officer Peak to manage it—he's the Narcologist. I'll return to the deck if he needs me."

The speakers were silent for a moment. Then Minx replied, "It's nothing you can't handle, Officer Crowley. Officer Peak is currently working on course plotting."

Memphys sighed, jabbing the air with a quick hook followed by an uppercut.

"Fine, I'll check it out," she said. Then, with a smirk, she added, "Oh, and Minx?"

"Yes, Officer Crowley?"

"Don't ever tell me what I can and can't manage, okay?"

The door to the prisoners' chamber hissed open as Memphys stepped inside, her hand resting lightly on her holstered weapon. The cold, sterile air prickled her skin as she called out, "Minx?"

Silence.

"Minx?" she called again, louder this time. "Damn it."

The chamber stretched in a perfect circle, its walls lined with icy capsules housing the ship's cargo—traitors and enemies of the Kaldrosdom. Memphys walked past the frozen bodies, their faces locked in peaceful oblivion behind frosted glass.

She laughed, the sound sharp and disdainful.

"Fools," she muttered, staring into the blank faces. "The Kaldros is our savior."

Turning slowly, she surveyed the capsules, each one a testament to the Kaldrosdom's dominance. Her voice echoed in the quiet chamber as she sneered, "I hope you all die."

A faint beeping broke the silence, drawing her attention. Memphys followed the sound around the curve of the room until she came upon the source. One of the chambers was open, its interior defrosted and empty.

Her breath hitched as she stared at the pile of fabric on the floor — the kind used to bind prisoners in stasis.

"My God," she whispered, her voice barely audible as her pulse thundered in her ears. The icy air seemed to thicken, each breath sharp and painful.

She turned to run, but her path was blocked. Standing before her was Vandar Manak, a prisoner from the Jupiter mines.

Reacting instinctively, Memphys lashed out with a kick, but Vandar moved to her side with practiced speed. He swept a leg behind hers and pushed her off balance. She tumbled backward, and before she could regain her footing, his hand closed around her throat.

She gasped as he forced her into the chamber, pinning her against the icy mattress. The stale air of the cryogenic pod filled her lungs as she struggled against his grip.

Vandar reached down and unholstered her gun.

"You will survive," he said, his voice steady. His eyes, however, betrayed a storm of emotions—regret, resolve, and a flicker of desperation.

Memphys looked up at him, her eyes wide with terror. Her confidence had vanished, replaced by the icy grip of fear.

"No!" she gasped, her voice cracking.

The chamber doors slammed shut with a cold finality.

The last thing Memphys heard was the sharp hiss of liquid nitrogen as frost began to creep across the glass. The pod's interior filled with blinding white vapor, muffling the world outside. Her eyes locked on Vandar, wide and unblinking, as the cold claimed her.

Vandar stepped back, his grip tightening on her weapon. He glanced around the chamber, his mind racing.

"This isn't over," he muttered under his breath.

24

Yotra thumped the console, his frustration mounting.

"Talk to me, Minx!" he yelled, his voice cutting through the silent bridge. His fingers flew across the keyboard as he attempted to diagnose the issue.

Nothing.

Minx's central unit appeared functional, but she remained unresponsive.

Suddenly, the ship shuddered, its motion slowing unnaturally.

"What the hell?" Yotra muttered, his eyes darting around the bridge. He glanced at the screens, which now flashed a single error message:

PROPULSION ERROR.

His heart pounded as Minx's voice abruptly returned, slicing through the tense silence.

"Gravatis has failed. Switching to thrusters."

A deep rumble vibrated through the ship, nearly knocking Yotra off balance. He stumbled back into the pilot seat, hastily buckling himself in as the vibrations intensified.

"Minx! Report! What is our distance from stray astral bodies?" he shouted over the noise.

"Course maintained. No astral bodies within six million kilometers," Minx replied calmly.

"Status?" he demanded, his voice taut.

"Apart from Gravatis failure, ship systems are optimal."

The rumbling began to subside, but the uneasy stillness that followed was worse. Yotra scanned the screens again, verifying Minx's assessment. Everything else seemed stable, but the loss of the Gravatis propulsion system left the ship sluggish, unstable—a sitting duck.

"Gravatis failure?" he muttered, incredulous. The system was supposed to be failsafe. This was unprecedented.

He paused, his fingers hovering over the console. "Where's Memphys?"

"Location of crew member Memphys Crowley is unknown," Minx replied flatly.

Yotra's frustration boiled over. "Don't fuck me around, Minx!" he snapped, rising from his seat.

As he turned to leave the bridge, he froze.

Standing in the doorway was Vandar Manak, Memphys's gun gripped tightly in his hand.

Yotra's mind raced. His eyes flicked between Vandar's weapon and his hardened expression. Acting on instinct, Yotra raised his hands slowly, keeping his voice steady.

"This ship is running on thrusters alone," he began, choosing his words carefully. "My ability to navigate is severely impaired. If you give me the gravity module back, I can reinstall it—and we can make sure the Kaldrosdom never knows about this."

Vandar didn't lower the gun. His expression was unreadable, his voice calm but firm.

"Shut up."

Yotra's chest tightened as he knelt to the floor, placing his hands on his head. The man looked calm—too calm—like someone who had already made peace with whatever came next. Yotra wasn't sure he could say the same for himself.

Vandar stepped closer, his tone icy. "Soon, the Kaldrosdom won't matter anymore. You're going to land this ship on Earth."

Yotra blinked, disbelief flashing across his face. "Landing on Earth with thrusters?" he asked, his voice rising. "Without a gravity module, our chances of not burning up are... maybe three in five—if that. There's a good chance it'll kill us all!"

Vandar didn't flinch. "That's the chance you're going to take. The longer we stay in space, the easier it'll be for your Kaldrosdom to track us."

He gestured with the gun, motioning for Yotra to stand.

Reluctantly, Yotra rose to his feet, his mind racing for a way out. "It'll take two days to reach Earth," he said, trying to keep his voice even.

"Two days is fine," Vandar replied coolly.

Yotra studied him, searching for a weakness. "If you're this desperate to escape," he ventured, "you've thought about what happens when the Kaldrosdom realizes you're missing. They'll come for you—and for me. No one gets away."

Vandar's mouth twitched into a grim smile as he raised his leg, revealing a device clasped around his ankle.

"You think I'm worried about what happens when they find me?" he said. "Two days. That's all you've got."

Vandar's gaze flicked briefly to the star-specked void visible through the bridge's viewport. Whatever he was planning, Yotra realized, it wasn't just about escape—it was bigger. Much bigger.

25

Yotra glanced over his shoulder at Vandar, slumped in restless sleep at the back of the flight deck. The fugitive twitched and muttered, his hands clenching as if he were still fighting some unseen enemy in his dreams.

Yotra turned his attention back to the clasp locked tightly around his ankle, chaining him to his flight seat. Escape was impossible. He had calculated every conceivable option, but nothing was remotely viable. Resisting Vandar wasn't just futile—it was suicidal.

His eyes flicked to the ship's monitors, where Memphys Crowley's frozen face stared back at him from inside her cryo-chamber. A glance at the vitals reassured him she was stable, though the logs showed she had entered the chamber in a state of panic. Her adrenaline, heart rate, and shock levels had been off the charts.

"At least she's alive," he muttered, exhaling sharply.

He glanced back to ensure Vandar was still asleep before pulling up the prisoner database on his console. Scrolling through files, he found his captor's record. His breath caught as he read the details.

"Vandar Manak... Unit Leader, Kaldros's Royal Army..." Yotra whispered, his eyes widening.

He had never encountered a prisoner like this. The Kaldros's men were notoriously loyal, conditioned to follow orders without hesitation—even to their deaths. For one of them to defect and end up on a prisoner transport? It was unthinkable.

A sudden scream shattered the silence. Yotra spun around to see Vandar bolt upright, drenched in sweat, his chest heaving. Quickly, Yotra closed the database and pretended to be focused on the navigation screen.

Vandar stalked toward him, rubbing his head as if trying to shake off the remnants of a nightmare.

"Are we nearing Earth?" Vandar asked, his voice groggy and rough.

Yotra hesitated, double-checking the coordinates on the screen. His brow furrowed in confusion.

"Earth's not there," he said, blinking in disbelief.

"What?" Vandar moved to Yotra's side, leaning over the console.

Yotra pointed at the map. "Based on the current date, orbital data, and star positions, Earth should be here." He tapped the screen. "But it's not. It's like it's… disappeared."

Vandar's expression remained calm. "It's there. Expand the map to the greater solar region."

Yotra hesitated. "But—"

"Do it."

Reluctantly, Yotra adjusted the map range. A new image appeared, revealing Earth's position—over 500,000 kilometers from where it should have been.

"How can that be?" Yotra asked, his voice tinged with disbelief.

Vandar smirked faintly. "You've just discovered something the Kaldrosdom doesn't want people like you to know. Set the new course."

Yotra turned to Vandar, his confusion morphing into suspicion. "What do you mean, 'people like me'? Tell me what's going on."

Vandar froze, his jaw tightening.

"If I tell you, the Kaldrosdom will have you killed," he said flatly.

He turned to walk away but stopped when Yotra didn't move. "Change the course," Vandar repeated, his voice hardening.

Yotra complied, adjusting the ship's trajectory. The vessel tilted slightly as it veered toward Earth's new position.

"You're different," Yotra said, glancing at Vandar. "How did you escape?"

Vandar studied him for a moment before stepping closer. "I'll tell you if you're unmarked by the Guild of Saturn."

"What?" Yotra recoiled as Vandar grabbed him by the neck, his fingers probing his throat.

"Stay still," Vandar ordered. "I'm checking for something."

Yotra froze, realizing Vandar wasn't strangling him but searching for something under his skin.

After a tense moment, Vandar released him. "You're unmarked."

Yotra rubbed his throat, glaring. "What the hell are you talking about?"

Vandar frowned. "You haven't been to Saturn, but you pilot a Kaldrosdom transport."

"I'll be taken eventually," Yotra admitted, "but the Genowan conflict has delayed routine screenings."

Vandar shook his head. "The Kaldros will never conquer Genowa," he said with certainty.

Yotra scoffed. "A man like you thinks he knows better than the Kaldros?"

Vandar's eyes narrowed. "Gravatis is the key to the Kaldros's power," he said. "In Genowa's green sun, Gravatis doesn't work. The Kaldrosdom's strength crumbles there."

Yotra stared, stunned by Vandar's knowledge.

"The Kaldros is an evil man, without balance," Vandar continued. "I see that now."

Yotra's voice softened. "You haven't told me how you escaped."

Vandar rolled up his sleeve, revealing a scar. "There's a chip under my skin. It overrode Minx, freed me, and misled you and your crew."

"Where did you get that technology?"

Vandar avoided the question, turning his gaze to the viewport. The blue-green sphere of Earth loomed closer.

Yotra switched tactics. "Why wasn't Earth where it should have been?"

Vandar's answer was calm but unsettling. "Earth is where it should be. We're the ones who aren't. We've traveled through time."

Yotra froze, his mind racing. "That's ridiculous."

"It's the truth," Vandar said. "The Kaldrosdom prevents time travel except when it serves their purpose. They've made you believe it's impossible."

"How did we do it?" Yotra asked, still struggling to process the revelation.

"By disengaging Gravatis at light-speed," Vandar explained. "The Kaldrosdom's failsafe systems reset ships to 'current time' when they drop below light-speed. I bypassed those safeguards."

Yotra was speechless. "So any ship with Gravatis can time travel?"

Vandar nodded.

Yotra's hands trembled as he adjusted the ship's course, aiming for the vast ocean below. "Well," he said, forcing a weak smile, "this might be the last time we see Earth alive."

The ship groaned under the strain, its frame shuddering violently as if trying to tear itself apart. Yotra's hands clenched the controls, his knuckles white. Vibrations rattled his teeth, and every fiber of his body screamed to abandon the descent.

The vessel swayed like a boat on a stormy sea. Its thrusters fired in rapid succession, struggling to stabilize the ship's descent. A fiery wall of plasma surrounded the hull, making the viewing screen too bright to look at directly.

"This is my first real thruster landing," Yotra muttered, flipping the emergency thrust controls.

"Your first?" Vandar asked, surprised.

"Well, who risks a spaceship when you have Gravatis?" Yotra shot back.

The ship's spin intensified, pitching them between space and the rapidly approaching Earth below. Yotra struggled to focus, his vision blurred by the dizzying horizon.

"Sky, Earth, sky, Earth..." he whispered, watching the chaotic spin.

For a fleeting moment, the horizon steadied. He slammed the lever back.

The thrusters roared, straining against the pull of gravity. The force slammed them into their seats as alarms blared. The ship bucked violently, its frame groaning under the pressure.

Yotra's vision darkened as the overwhelming G-forces pinned him down. The last thing he heard before blacking out was Minx's voice, calm and indifferent:

"Unable to find vector for thrust."

26

Yotra stirred, the fugitive's voice pulling him from the depths of unconsciousness.

"As a kid, I loved the sea. Isn't it beautiful?" Vandar's voice was calm, almost wistful, cutting through the haze of Yotra's groggy mind.

Blinking against the harsh sunlight streaming through the emergency hatch, Yotra winced as the brightness stung his eyes. Through the haze, he made out Vandar, standing near the open door, a cigarette dangling between his fingers. The smoke curled around him, framing the vast ocean beyond. Waves sparkled like a sea of stars, an endless expanse of blue stretching to the horizon.

"You managed to get the ship into a decent re-entry vector," Vandar continued, his tone conversational. "Minx did the rest. For a while, I thought we were done for. You were out cold, and that damned computer didn't seem to be doing anything useful." He exhaled a plume of smoke, the cigarette's glow briefly illuminating his face. "But once the flames subsided, I realized we weren't plummeting anymore. We leveled out, skimming along the sea instead of crashing into it. My God, what a relief."

Vandar flicked the cigarette out the hatch, watching it vanish into the ocean below. Then he turned, walking toward Yotra, who was still slumped in the pilot's seat.

"How's your concussion?" Vandar asked, his tone almost casual.

Yotra didn't respond. His head throbbed, and the world still felt unsteady beneath him.

Vandar shrugged. "You'll live." He nodded toward Yotra's feet. "You're free. The clasp is off."

Yotra glanced down, blinking in confusion as he noticed the device that had locked him to the seat was indeed gone. Relief mingled with suspicion as he raised his gaze back to Vandar, only to feel a sudden sharp prick in his arm.

A soft hiss followed.

"What the hell—" Yotra's words slurred as his vision swam. He struggled to push himself upright, using Vandar's arm as leverage, but his body refused to cooperate.

"You bastard," he muttered, his voice weak. "What did you..."

Before he could finish, his strength gave out, and he collapsed back into the seat.

Vandar stepped back, watching him with a faint smirk. "Don't worry. It's nothing lethal—just enough to make sure you get some rest. I need a head start."

Yotra's eyelids grew heavier, his vision narrowing into a blur.

"You'll stay here and wait for your precious Kaldrosdom to come and collect you," Vandar said. He turned and headed toward the equipment stores, his boots echoing softly against the metallic floor.

Vandar moved with purpose, rummaging through the storage compartments near the flight deck. He grabbed what he needed—a black climbing harness, food supplies, a medical kit, and a holster for Memphys's laser pistol, which he strapped securely to his side.

From behind him, Yotra's groggy voice broke the silence. "You think... you can... run forever?"

Vandar chuckled, his tone low and calm. "Not forever. Just long enough."

He slung the backpack over his shoulder, securing it tightly. "They'll catch up eventually, but the margin of error in time travel makes it unlikely they'll arrive within weeks—or even months—of our landing."

He walked back to the flight deck, standing near the slumbering Yotra. The pilot's head had lolled to the side, his breathing deep and steady as the sedative took full effect.

"They're not here now," Vandar muttered, half to himself. "Which means they won't arrive before us. Funny thing, time travel."

He reached over to the console, pressing a series of buttons. Outside, the spaceship's exterior shimmered briefly before vanishing completely.

"No need to alarm the locals," Vandar said, glancing at Yotra one last time.

He stepped to the open emergency hatch, pausing to take in the view. The waves crashed below, their rhythm steady and eternal. Vandar took a deep breath, the salty air filling his lungs.

With one final glance over his shoulder, he disappeared into the horizon, leaving the cloaked ship and its sleeping pilot behind.

27

When Yotra awoke, he felt barely alive. His head throbbed with a relentless ache, and his thoughts were sluggish, as if his brain had been submerged in a dense fog. Staggering to his feet, he made his way down the corridor to the cryo-chambers, leaning on the walls for support.

Reaching Memphys Crowley's chamber, he placed a hand on the frosted glass and studied her face, frozen in suspended animation. He glanced at the status panel beside the chamber, the steady green light reassuring him.

"You're still alive," he murmured, a small wave of relief washing over him.

He pressed the necessary buttons to initiate the defrost sequence. The hum of machinery filled the room as the process began.

"Minx?" Yotra called out, his voice hoarse.

"Responding," came her robotic, monotone reply.

"How long before Officer Crowley is fully revived from stasis?"

"Twenty-two hours," Minx replied flatly.

Yotra frowned, glancing at the other chambers. He gestured toward them. "Status of the remaining capsules?"

"All chambers are intact and functioning. The occupants remain in stable cryogenic sleep."

He walked past the capsules, his eyes lingering on the faces locked behind the icy barriers. Civilians, traitors, rebels—all trapped in a state of frozen limbo. They were alive, but their fates seemed no more certain than his own.

Satisfied, he turned and left the chamber. There was no reason to disturb them.

The ship rocked gently with the rhythm of the waves. From the open emergency hatch, Yotra gazed out at the shoreline less than a hundred meters away. The white sand shimmered under the morning sun, a stark contrast to the metallic gloom of the spacecraft.

He stood at the hatch, a hastily packed bag of provisions slung over his shoulder. Inside were the essentials: food, water, a medkit, and a knife. The waterproof seals were double-checked. His breathing was shallow, his hands trembling slightly.

"This is madness," he muttered to himself.

Vandar Manak had nearly a half-day lead on him. A trained soldier with a laser weapon and years of combat experience, Vandar was an opponent Yotra had no chance of defeating. But none of that mattered. Vandar had stolen Gravatis, the Kaldrosdom's most closely guarded technological secret.

Gravatis wasn't just a propulsion device—it was the very cornerstone of the Kaldrosdom's dominance. If Vandar delivered it to the Genowans or anyone else, it would tilt the balance of power in the universe. Yotra's mind raced with the possible consequences.

It wasn't just duty or loyalty driving him—it was survival. The Kaldrosdom didn't tolerate failure, especially when it came to safeguarding Gravatis. If Yotra let Vandar slip away, he would be labeled a traitor. The execution would be swift and merciless.

He glanced back at the interior of the ship one last time. Memphys would wake up to find his note. It wasn't much, but it explained his decision.

He turned back to the horizon.

"No more time to waste," he muttered.

The deep blue waters stretched out before him, vast and endless. He stood at the edge of the emergency hatch, staring down at the sea. The sheer quantity of water was overwhelming—he had never seen anything like it. He hesitated for a moment, unsure.

"I can swim... somewhat," he said to himself, as if the words could bolster his confidence.

Securing the bag tightly to his back, he took a deep breath and leapt from the hatch into the salty water below.

The plunge startled him. Instead of the icy cold he had braced himself for, the water was surprisingly warm. It wrapped around him like a living current, buoyant and unfamiliar. His arms and legs moved instinctively, propelling him toward the distant shore.

With each stroke, the ship behind him grew smaller, its silhouette blending into the endless blue horizon. Ahead, the sand glimmered like a beacon of hope—or perhaps danger.

Yotra swam onward, the weight of his mission pulling at him like an anchor.

28

She awoke with a scream. Cold and drenched in clear mucus, her body trembled uncontrollably. As she tried to sit up, a wave of nausea overwhelmed her, forcing her to gag. Instinctively, she turned her head to the floor and vomited, the retching leaving her weak and shivering.

For a moment, she stayed hunched over, breath ragged. Another coughing fit followed, expelling more mucus and bile. Weak and disoriented, she crawled to a clean part of the floor and collapsed onto her side, gasping for air.

Her head throbbed with relentless intensity. Clutching her temples, she tried to focus, piecing together fragments of memory.

Above her loomed a circle of encapsulated figures. Recognition dawned, sharp and bitter. The cryo-chamber.

Memories surged back: the man who had overpowered her, the brutal fight, the searing pain of liquid nitrogen spray as she was frozen alive.

"I'll kill the bastard," she hissed through clenched teeth.

Her eyes fell on the capsule she'd tumbled out of. At its base lay a small red spray can. She recognized it immediately: Isoprotonitrate spray, a potent painkiller and anti-nausea agent. With trembling hands, she snatched it and sprayed two long bursts under her tongue.

Relief came quickly. The pounding in her skull dulled, and her nausea subsided. She leaned back against the wall, breathing deeply as her strength returned.

"Yotra must have left it," she muttered, her voice hoarse.

She scanned the room, but there was no sign of him. Frustration simmered beneath her exhaustion. For several minutes, she sat against the wall, gathering herself.

When she finally stood, it was slow and deliberate. She staggered to her capsule and slammed the door shut with a force that rattled the chamber.

"Fucking thing!" she yelled, her voice echoing in the sterile room.

"Minx!" she barked.

"Yes, Officer Crowley," the ship's robotic voice responded smoothly.

"Where are we?"

"Earth," Minx replied flatly.

Memphys froze, her mind racing to process the word. "Earth?" she repeated, disbelief dripping from her tone.

"Yes," Minx confirmed. "The ship landed using emergency thrusters. It is still without its Gravatis device."

The words hit her like a punch to the gut. "We've lost Gravatis?!" she shouted, panic tightening her chest.

Gravatis wasn't just vital—it was sacred. Its loss wasn't just negligence; it was treason. Her mind raced, imagining the Kaldrosdom's wrath.

"Oh, my God," she whispered, running a trembling hand through her damp hair.

"Officer Peak has left a report on the bridge console," Minx added.

Memphys stood frozen, the full weight of her situation pressing down on her. She wasn't just facing failure—she was staring down death. The Kaldrosdom wouldn't forgive her for losing Gravatis.

She clenched her fists, forcing herself to focus. She needed to act quickly to salvage what she could. Her gaze swept over the icy capsules surrounding her, the prisoners locked inside their frozen tombs.

"The prisoners..." she began, her voice faltering.

"All intact and in stasis," Minx replied. "No faults detected."

Memphys's jaw tightened. Loose ends weren't an option. If even one prisoner escaped or fell into enemy hands, her life was over.

"Terminate them all," she said coldly.

Minx was silent for a moment, processing the command.

"Terminate!" Memphys screamed, slamming her fist against the wall. "Did you hear me, you piece of—"

"Termination protocol initiated," Minx interrupted.

The capsules lit up, their icy interiors flashing with ominous red lights. The hum of machinery grew louder as the chambers began heating rapidly. Mist swirled around Memphys's feet, thick and cold, as the process began.

"Instruction order logged: Officer Memphys Crowley," Minx said.

The capsules emitted synchronized beeps, their lights growing brighter as the haze filled the room.

"Rationale for termination requested, Officer Crowley," Minx prompted.

Memphys shifted uncomfortably, her feet shuffling against the cold floor. Her gaze flicked to the capsules, now obscured by swirling mist. She took a deep breath, standing straighter as she steeled herself.

"Unanticipated events," she said, her voice clipped and mechanical. "Emergency landing and terrorist attack. Terminate prisoners to prevent collateral damage."

"Rationale accepted," Minx confirmed.

Memphys turned on her heel and strode out of the chamber, her steps quick and deliberate. Behind her, the capsules hissed and crackled as their occupants disappeared into the smoky mist.

29

Yotra concluded that Manak would head for the nearest settlement. The fugitive's best chance of escape lay in finding transport, and despite not knowing the exact year they had landed in, Yotra was certain Manak would make a beeline for civilization.

His fear of the Kaldrosdom's wrath drove him forward. The thought of returning empty-handed gnawed at him—a fate far worse than the exhaustion clawing at his legs or the blistering sun beating down on his back. He pressed on, ignoring the ache in his muscles and the tightness in his chest.

His pilot's uniform, now dry, clung uncomfortably to his skin, the salt from the seawater chafing at his neck. Judging by the oppressive heat, he guessed it couldn't possibly be winter. Yet the trees and plants surrounding him didn't suggest a tropical climate either. The world felt eerily familiar and alien all at once.

He recalled the ship's trajectory during their descent. They had been heading toward the Mediterranean region, but beyond that, his knowledge of Earth's geography was woefully inadequate. The sparse landscape provided no clear answers, leaving him adrift in both time and place.

Yotra adjusted the straps of his climbing harness, a grim reminder of the stakes. If Vandar Manak had activated Gravatis, he could be anywhere—or on the verge of making himself unreachable. The device wasn't just advanced; it was powerful enough to tip the balance of the

Kaldrosdom's tightly controlled empire. Losing it would mean certain death for Yotra.

He pulled out a prisoner beacon receiver and switched it on, the small screen blinking to life. The device would pick up a signal if Manak came within a 30-kilometer radius. For now, it was frustratingly silent, its emptiness gnawing at his nerves.

He adjusted the settings, and for a fleeting moment, he thought he saw a faint blip. His breath caught, but the signal vanished just as quickly. Was it interference, or had Vandar come briefly into range? He couldn't be sure.

The silence around him was oppressive. The rustle of unseen creatures in the brush and the faint crackle of dry earth beneath his boots amplified the sense of isolation. Each step felt heavier than the last, the weight of the air pressing down on him like an invisible hand.

Yotra clenched his teeth, his resolve hardening. Vandar Manak wasn't just an escaped prisoner—he was a soldier, trained and dangerous, carrying the most valuable technology in the Kaldrosdom. Yotra had no illusions about what might happen if he caught up to the fugitive, but the alternative—facing the Kaldrosdom's wrath—was far worse.

He looked ahead at the seemingly endless stretch of wilderness. His mind wavered, questioning whether this pursuit was even possible. But he forced his doubts aside. Failure wasn't an option.

Gripping the receiver tighter, he kept moving, scanning the horizon for any sign of the man he had to stop.

30

Memphys listened to Yotra's message, her hands trembling with anger.

"Could anything else possibly go wrong?" she spat through clenched teeth.

As Yotra's image disappeared from the screen, her rage boiled over. Her fists tightened, and she let out a blood-curdling scream, slamming them down onto the console with a force that made the panels creak under the impact. Her knuckles throbbed, but she didn't care. She stood there for a moment, chest heaving, trying to gather her spiraling thoughts.

"A New Kaldrosdom Message has been received," Minx's robotic voice interrupted.

Memphys froze, her pulse quickening. "What message?" she demanded, turning toward the screen.

"Hastacer Kaldrosdom Ship, HKS-47, has made contact," Minx continued calmly. "It will arrive here in two hours."

Memphys's eyes widened. "A Hastacer ship? That's a royal transport, isn't it?"

"Confirmed," Minx replied. "A Carnos flagship."

Her blood ran cold. The Carnos were the Kaldros's most elite forces, merciless enforcers of his will. Their arrival didn't mean help—it meant judgment.

"Oh, sweet God," Memphys whispered, stumbling back from the

console. The steady hum of the ship seemed to grow louder in her ears, like a drumbeat heralding her doom.

She pressed her hands against her temples, trying to focus. "Think, damn it. Think!"

"Dump the prisoners," she said abruptly, her voice shaking with urgency.

Minx paused. "Dumping the cargo will place them in the sea. Are you sure you—"

"Just do it!" Memphys screamed, cutting the AI off.

"Affirmative," Minx replied.

The bridge felt stifling, the dim lights flickering slightly as the ship swayed gently in the waves. Memphys's mind raced, the weight of her situation pressing on her chest like a vice.

Would dumping the prisoners be enough? Or would the Carnos see her as just another loose end to tie up? The thought gnawed at her, but she shoved it aside. There was no time for doubt.

She turned on her heel and stormed off the bridge. She had to prepare for their arrival. The Carnos didn't negotiate. They didn't forgive. And Memphys knew that if she made even the slightest misstep, they wouldn't hesitate to destroy her.

31

After two days of hiking, Yotra received the signal from his target. Vandar Manak was within five kilometers. He checked his scanner and noted the human settlement twenty kilometers away. Picking up his pace, Yotra hoped to intercept Manak before he reached the settlement. His pilot's uniform, now dry in the relentless sun, clung to him as he trudged onward, the fear of the Kaldrosdom's wrath driving him forward despite his exhaustion.

"One kilometer away," Yotra muttered, glancing at the scanner as he scanned the forested valley ahead. He raised his laser rifle, surveying the dense terrain through his rangefinder. Hills and trees stretched into the distance, and beyond them, he could just make out the settlement—a cluster of stone buildings.

"What year am I even in?" he wondered, his thoughts briefly drifting before he refocused on his surroundings. The scanner beeped again, confirming Vandar's proximity. Yotra moved cautiously downhill, his rifle slung over his back and his laser pistol now in hand for agility.

"Eight hundred meters," he whispered, heart pounding as the signal grew stronger. He weaved between the trees, his movements precise, each step deliberate.

Suddenly, the signal stopped. Yotra froze. "Shit," he hissed. "He knows I'm here."

Dropping into a crouch behind a tree, Yotra surveyed the clearing ahead. The open space offered little cover, with only a few tall trees standing defiantly in the sunlit expanse. He flicked off his pistol's safety, readying the climbing harness he carried—a precaution if Vandar attempted to use Gravatis. But as he watched, something unexpected happened. The pebbles around his boots began to roll, shifting as though pulled by an invisible force.

"What the—?" Yotra exclaimed, his voice barely above a whisper. He suddenly felt weightless, his balance failing as gravity itself seemed to betray him. His body lifted off the ground, flying horizontally across the clearing.

"Gravatis," he realized, panic surging as he tumbled through the air. The world spun violently, and he caught a glimpse of a massive tree looming ahead. There was no time to brace before he slammed into it with bone-jarring force. The impact knocked the rifle from its strap, and gravity returned to normal, sending him crashing to the dusty ground below.

Dazed and gasping for air, Yotra barely registered the sound of laughter. He blinked through the haze of pain, his blurred vision catching the figure of Vandar Manak approaching. The fugitive's footsteps were measured, deliberate. Yotra clawed at the ground, his fingers scraping against the soil as he reached for his fallen pistol.

"Don't bother," Vandar said, his voice laced with amusement. The pistol slid away from Yotra's grasp, seemingly of its own accord. It rebounded off a rock and floated upward, hovering mid-air before drifting into Vandar's outstretched hand. He inspected it briefly, then aimed it at Yotra's head.

"What made you think chasing me alone was a good idea?" Vandar asked, his tone mocking yet calm.

Yotra coughed, clutching his ribs. "I had no choice."

Vandar chuckled, lowering the pistol slightly. "You're lucky I'm feeling generous."

Yotra's eyes darted toward his rifle, but Vandar noticed. With a casual motion, he kicked it farther away. He then pulled out a small black device—Gravatis—its interface displaying force vectors and directional data.

"Amazing, isn't it?" Vandar said, almost to himself. "Gravatis powers everything: the Kaldros's fleets, the Carnos' abilities, even the manipulation of time itself. All from one device. And now, it's mine."

"You...you stole it from the ship?" Yotra wheezed, still struggling to stand.

Vandar smirked. "Liberated it. Usually, Gravatis is rigged to self-destruct if disconnected. But let's just say I had some help bypassing that little safeguard."

"Why?" Yotra demanded, his voice hoarse. "What are you planning?"

Vandar's expression darkened. "To end the Kaldros's tyranny."

Yotra finally managed to stand, though unsteadily. "And you think Gravatis will be enough?"

Vandar shrugged. "It's a start. Now, let's finish this." He adjusted the pistol's settings, activating its self-destruct mode. A robotic voice counted down: "Ten, nine, eight..."

Vandar tossed the pistol into the trees, where it vanished among the foliage. "Seven, six..." Yotra turned and ran, Vandar following suit as the countdown continued.

"Two, one..." The explosion rocked the clearing, a blinding flash of light and a deafening roar scattering ash and debris. The ground trembled, and Yotra hit the dirt, shielding his head as waves of heat washed over him.

When the chaos subsided, Yotra lifted his head. The clearing was engulfed in smoke, the trees ablaze. He coughed, the air thick with ash. In the distance, he saw Vandar disappearing into the haze.

"You'd better leave me be, Officer," Vandar called over his shoulder. "I have no quarrel with you. Go back to your ship."

Yotra watched helplessly as Vandar vanished into the smoky inferno. His lungs burned, and he tore a strip from his shirt to cover his mouth. Staggering to his feet, he stumbled toward the distant blue of the sky, desperate to escape the suffocating smoke.

<h1 style="text-align:center">32</h1>

Memphys stood at the emergency hatch, staring at the empty sky. The afternoon sun blazed in a cloudless expanse, but her mind was storming. She brushed a piece of lint off her uniform, checking her badges and holster one last time. Every detail had to be perfect. If anything went wrong, there wouldn't be a second chance.

The beach ahead of the ship was still deserted, a stretch of unbroken sand. Beyond it, the forest loomed dark and quiet, untouched by human hands. She glanced down at the ship's reflection in the gently rippling sea. Half-submerged, its sleek hull floated like a sleeping predator. She focused on the horizon, straining her eyes against the brightness.

A low rumble broke the silence. Memphys's breath caught.

"They're here," she whispered.

The sky ahead began to shimmer. The air itself seemed to ripple as if reality was bending. The blue deepened into silver, and the outline of a ship materialized from the void. Its sleek, weaponized silhouette emerged with ominous grace, smaller than hers but unmistakably royal.

Spray erupted from the sea as the ship stabilized. A door on its side slid open, extending a gangplank towards her own hatch with smooth, mechanical precision. Memphys braced herself.

A single figure stepped out.

He was a Carnos, the Kaldros's Royal Guard. His armor gleamed black under the sun, and a crimson cape billowed behind him. A curved dagger hung from his belt, his hand resting on its hilt with practiced ease. Slung over his shoulder were the infamous fire orbs, their dormant glow a warning of the destruction he could unleash.

The Carnos stopped halfway down the gangplank and turned his head toward the water. Memphys followed his gaze. Floating near her ship's hull was one of the prisoners she had dumped earlier. The armored man extended a hand.

To her shock, the body rose from the water, spinning slowly in mid-air. It floated closer, the Carnos inspecting it with morbid curiosity. Then, with a flick of his wrist, he released it. The corpse fell back into the sea with a sickening splash.

Another Carnos appeared behind the first, striding onto the plank with equal menace.

Memphys stepped back instinctively.

The sound of metal heels echoed as a third figure emerged from the ship. Memphys's stomach turned to ice.

The figure was not human but a silver machine adorned in royal purple. His articulated limbs moved fluidly, the metal etched with intricate ornamentation. His glowing eyes scanned the ship, and though his expressionless face betrayed no emotion, his presence exuded authority.

It was Ilores, the Kaldros's companion of over a thousand years.

Memphys froze as he stepped onto the gangplank. She knew better than to speak without being addressed. Ilores moved with calm precision, his gaze surveying the bridge as though weighing its worth.

Finally, his glowing eyes settled on her.

"Report, Officer." His voice was calm, his words meticulously enunciated.

She swallowed hard. "My Lord, one of the prisoners, Vandar Manak, took control of the ship's systems through unknown means. He has since escaped."

"Escaped," Ilores repeated, his tone neutral.

"Yes, my Lord."

"And how did this ship arrive in the past?"

"I—" Memphys hesitated. "I don't know. He froze me in a Narco-chamber and—"

"Vandar Manak has knowledge of the hidden capabilities of Gravatis," Ilores interrupted, his eyes narrowing slightly. "Where is he now?"

Memphys steadied her voice. "The pilot, Officer Yotra Peak, is in pursuit."

Ilores turned his gaze to the horizon, his hands clasped behind his back. The Carnos stood like statues at his sides.

"Leave them here," Ilores said finally. "It will not matter."

Memphys's heart skipped a beat. Was he condemning her too?

Ilores turned to her, placing a cold metal hand on her shoulder.

"You are fortunate," he said. "I am entrusting you with a mission for the Kaldrosdom."

She looked up at him, trying to mask her fear.

"You will remain here, in this time, to recover Gravatis and destroy it."

Her stomach lurched. "But my Lord, if I destroy Gravatis, I'll be trapped here forever!"

Ilores tilted his head, studying her. Then, with an unnervingly gentle gesture, he stroked her cheek with his metal fingers.

"You will be rewarded," he said. "The Kaldrosdom will return for you, and you shall be knighted at the Guild of Saturn."

She bowed deeply. "Thank you, my Lord."

Ilores handed her a small device.

"This will track Gravatis's signal. Use it wisely. The Kaldrosdom's future depends on your success."

Memphys gripped the device tightly. "I will not fail."

Ilores stepped back, nodding once before turning toward the gangplank. The Carnos followed silently, their capes trailing behind them.

Memphys stood at the hatch, watching as Ilores disappeared into the silver ship. The gangplank retracted with a mechanical hiss, and the ship melted back into the void, the horizon returning to blue.

She stared at the empty sky for a long moment, the weight of the device in her hand.

"I'll show you, Vandar Manak," she muttered. "You'll regret crossing me."

33

Yotra's blind retreat through the choking smoke brought him to a sudden halt. The ground stopped at a crumbling edge, dropping into a steep, hazy abyss. He squinted into the murky void below but couldn't see where the edge led or how far it fell. The acrid smoke burned his throat and filled his lungs, its heaviness pressing against his chest like a weight. He coughed violently, clutching at his ribs, and peered along the ridge, desperate for an alternative path.

He staggered along the edge, searching for another way, but his legs gave out beneath him. He fell to his knees, coughing harder now, his vision blurring. The sharp crackle of stones dislodging beneath his hands startled him, and he looked over the edge, watching them disappear into the dense fog below.

"No choice," he rasped, his voice barely audible in the deafening roar of the fire. His fingers clawed at the dirt, trembling. With a deep, shuddering breath, he rolled himself over the edge, praying that something merciful awaited him below.

The world blurred into chaos as he plummeted through the smoke. A jarring impact slammed into his shoulder, and he felt himself tumbling, rolling down a steep slope. Dirt and rocks battered his body, and he curled into a ball, shielding his head as best he could. The descent seemed endless until, finally, he slid to a stop on a flat stretch of ground. Gasping, he lay still, the clean, cool air a shock after the oppressive fumes above.

He blinked up at the swirling smoke that loomed over the slope. Relief was short-lived, however, as a low rumble broke through the quiet. The sound of shifting stones, heavy and deliberate, sent a chill down his spine. He strained to lift his head, his muscles aching, and his eyes stung from the smoke. The outline of a vehicle emerged through the haze—a large, lumbering machine with a cockpit behind a growling motor.

Yotra tried to move, but his body refused to cooperate. The vehicle slowed and stopped in front of him. The door creaked open, and a stocky man climbed out, his silhouette framed by the pale sunlight. The man's round face was red and sweaty, his grey eyebrows furrowed with concern as he hurried toward Yotra, yelling in a language Yotra didn't understand.

Yotra flinched as the man knelt beside him, his hands rough but not unkind. The man gestured urgently toward the burning hillside and tugged at Yotra's arm, urging him to his feet. Dizzy and disoriented, Yotra staggered, leaning heavily on the stranger as they stumbled toward the back of the vehicle. The man hoisted him onto a pile of sacks in the covered bed of the transport and hurried back to the cockpit.

The engine growled louder as the vehicle lurched forward, the vibrations jarring Yotra's bruised body. He let his head fall back against the sacks, closing his eyes as exhaustion washed over him. The cool breeze on his face was a welcome reprieve, and he focused on the rhythmic motion of the vehicle, letting it soothe his frayed nerves.

The transport rattled along the gravel road, bouncing over tight corners. When it finally turned onto a smoother, paved path, Yotra opened his eyes. The forest had given way to a small settlement, its buildings simple and made of stone or concrete. People moved hurriedly through the streets, their bright, loose clothing in stark contrast to his dark, fitted uniform. He shrank back instinctively, aware of how conspicuous he must look.

The transport came to a halt in the town's center, and Yotra climbed down from the truck bed, brushing dust from his uniform. He scanned his surroundings, noting the crowd's agitation. Many carried bundles of belongings, their faces tense with worry. Two red vehicles with ladders and hoses roared past, their wailing sirens piercing the air as they sped toward the fire.

The stocky driver appeared beside him again, gesturing emphatically toward a large building across the road. Yotra hesitated, trying to decipher the man's rapid words, but the driver began pushing him toward the structure. Reluctantly, Yotra followed, weaving through the crowd.

Inside, the building was packed with people jostling each other in their urgency to move forward. The air buzzed with frantic chatter, the tension palpable. A man in a blue uniform blew a whistle sharply, directing the crowd toward a long concrete platform. Yotra allowed himself to be carried along, his confusion growing with each step.

At the platform's edge, Yotra stopped, staring in awe at the scene before him. A train stood waiting, its carriages a curious mix of wood and metal. Unlike the sleek, efficient machines of his time, this train looked outdated, almost quaint. Its head faced a dark tunnel carved into the rock, the only visible path out of the valley.

The uniformed man blew his whistle again, urging the crowd onto the train. Smoke was already creeping into the edges of the settlement, its ominous tendrils a stark reminder of the advancing fire. Yotra glanced back at the burning hillside and felt a pang of helplessness. There was no going back.

He moved to the rear of the train, finding an empty spot in one of the less crowded carriages. As the train lurched forward, its electric hum mingling with the passengers' murmurs, Yotra folded his arms and leaned against the wall. He felt the weight of his situation settle over him. Stranded in a foreign time, with no clear plan and no way to contact his ship, he could only hope that the next stop would bring some clarity—and a chance to regroup.

34

Half an hour passed, and the train rattled through various stations without stopping. Yotra caught a glimpse of a station sign: *MONTE ROSSO*. The cabin buzzed with conversation, the passengers' voices loud and relentless.

He stared at the people around him, gesturing animatedly as if yelling was their natural tone of speech. The elderly couple next to him seemed to be locked in a heated exchange, their wrinkled faces alive with passion. The woman clutched a caged rooster in her trembling hands, while the man guarded a battered leather suitcase. Their sun-weathered skin spoke of long days under a blazing sun. Around them, younger passengers—muscular men in soiled work clothes and women in aprons—seemed equally engrossed in chatter.

Yotra looked out the window, tuning out the noise. The train climbed higher, winding through mountainous terrain, its tracks curling around steep slopes and crossing bridges that spanned deep ravines. He scanned the horizon for signs of the next station but saw only endless tracks and the yawning chasm below.

The carriage door creaked open, and a man stepped inside.

"Vandar Manak!" Yotra muttered, startled.

He ducked behind the elderly woman and her rooster, but the movement caught no one's attention—least of all Vandar, who was making his way toward the rear of the carriage. Yotra's pulse quickened. This was his chance.

Quickly, he untied the rope on his harness, readying it for an attack.

Vandar passed within reach. Yotra lunged, looping the rope around Vandar's neck. The woman screamed as Vandar staggered, instinctively backing into the rear door. The impact cracked the wood, and Yotra grunted, holding tight as Vandar gasped for air.

The passengers scattered, retreating toward the front of the carriage. Vandar swung wildly, slamming Yotra into a seat. The rope cut into his neck, but Vandar clawed at it, managing to loosen the hold just enough to breathe.

"Let me go!" Vandar rasped.

"Not unless you agree to return to the ship and give back Gravatis!" Yotra barked.

Vandar managed a strangled laugh. "Never."

With a fierce twist, Vandar backed into the rear door again. The cracked wood splintered further, the glass shattering into shards. Yotra risked a glance behind them. The tracks stretched below, blurring past at dizzying speed. Beyond the bridge, a river snaked far below —a lethal drop.

"Stop!" Yotra yelled.

"You stop!" Vandar shot back, his voice hoarse.

Another impact, and the door gave way. Yotra's body pitched through the opening, his grip on the rope slipping. He tumbled into open air.

For a heart-stopping moment, he fell freely. His stomach lurched, and he braced for the unforgiving tracks below. Then the harness jerked tight, halting his descent. The wind roared in his ears as he dangled, suspended in the void.

He looked down. The tracks zipped by far below, but he wasn't being dragged. He was floating, tethered to Vandar.

"Gravatis!" Yotra realized, looking up at Vandar, who clung to the rope, bracing himself against the carriage walls.

Vandar glanced down, sweat streaming from his face. His grip on the rope was slipping. Desperately, he scanned the carriage for something to tie it to but found nothing.

"Lasciami aiutarti!" a woman's voice called.

Vandar whipped his head around. A young woman was running

toward him, her words hurried.

"Let me help you!" she repeated, switching to English.

Vandar hesitated but gestured to the rope. The woman grabbed it, adding her strength to his. Together, they began pulling Yotra back toward the train.

The carriage shuddered violently, and a deafening explosion rocked the train.

"Blaster fire!" Vandar thought, alarmed.

The wheels screeched as flames erupted along the undercarriage. The train swayed dangerously, threatening to derail. The young woman lost her footing and toppled into Vandar, nearly dragging him toward the open door. The rope slipped from his grasp, and Yotra plunged into the abyss.

Vandar didn't have time to react. The burning carriage groaned as it broke away from the train, tilting precariously before it tipped into the ravine. Acting on instinct, Vandar grabbed the girl and leapt from the collapsing car.

They plummeted through the air. Vandar held the screaming woman tightly, the wind tearing at their clothes. Below them, Yotra hit the river with a thunderous splash, disappearing beneath the surface.

Vandar reached for Gravatis, but the rushing water was too close. With no other choice, he closed his eyes and braced for impact as the river surged toward them.

35

They plunged into the frigid depths, the impact knocking the air from their lungs as the icy water enveloped them. Vandar felt the crushing pressure in his ears and chest as they descended into the dark, murky abyss. The girl hung limp in his arms. He tightened his grip and began swimming toward the surface, the distant circle of light a faint beacon above.

Each stroke was a battle against exhaustion and the weight of his soaked clothing. Halfway to the surface, the girl stirred and panicked, thrashing in the water and dragging them downward. Vandar held her firmly, his arms aching, and propelled them both upward with determined kicks.

The light grew brighter, and Vandar's instincts screamed that the surface was near. His lungs burned, but he refused to let go of her. Then, suddenly, his hand broke free into the air.

Vandar gulped down a desperate breath, savoring the sharp taste of oxygen. He laid the girl atop his chest, her face clear of the water. The waves rocked them violently, forcing him to swallow water between gasps.

"Please," he thought, "breathe."

She coughed, expelling water from her lungs, and then inhaled deeply. Relief flooded him as she began to sob and gasp for air. Vandar kicked toward the edge of the lagoon, his legs trembling with every motion.

They reached the shallows, where the girl scrambled onto the rocky shore, collapsing in a trembling heap. Vandar, chest heaving, stayed in the water a moment longer, his feet steady on the riverbed. He coughed up the last of the water from his lungs and looked around.

The remains of the train carriage lay submerged in the lagoon, its charred edges blackened by blaster fire. Vandar studied the jagged burn marks, his mind racing.

"Who was firing at us?" he muttered.

He scanned the shoreline and spotted Yotra clinging to a boulder near a waterfall. The space pilot's hands were wrapped tightly around the rock, his body hunched as though he feared the river would swallow him whole. Vandar waded through the shallow rapids, his eyes locked on the boulder.

"Yotra!" he yelled, his voice barely audible over the roar of the waterfall.

There was no response. Vandar called again, louder this time, but the rushing water drowned out his words. The girl, now standing unsteadily, began to follow him, her expression wary. Suddenly, someone seized her from behind.

She froze as cold steel pressed against her neck.

"Don't move," a woman's voice growled.

Yotra glanced up, hearing faint shouting over the waterfall's roar. He turned to see Vandar approaching through the shallow water. Rising shakily to his feet, Yotra braced himself against the rock and watched the fugitive draw closer.

Vandar stopped a few meters away, his palms raised in a gesture of peace.

"I haven't changed my offer," Vandar called out. "Leave me be and live. Escape the Kaldrosdom with me! You're free here."

"I will never be free!" Yotra shouted back, his voice raw. "If I don't return you to my ship with Gravatis reinstalled, I'll be killed! The Kaldrosdom doesn't forgive failure."

Vandar stepped closer, his tone firm but imploring. "Here, in this time, the Kaldrosdom can't reach you. You're free. This world is better than the one we left behind."

Yotra hesitated, his gaze shifting to the idyllic surroundings—the crystalline water, the lush greenery, the towering cliffs. Could this really be a refuge from the Kaldrosdom's grasp?

"And how do I live here?" Yotra asked, his voice trembling. "How do I escape my past?"

Vandar fixed him with a determined look. "You don't escape it — you live with it. The Kaldrosdom's time gates will reset everything. Every year, on New Year's Day, time is corrected. Everything reverts to the path it was meant to follow, as if we were never here. The Kaldrosdom won't find you."

Yotra blinked in astonishment. "Time gates?"

Vandar nodded. "They're the key to the Kaldrosdom's power. They erase our disruptions and maintain their control."

Yotra took a step forward, his resolve softening. "And you're sure? The Kaldrosdom won't find us here?"

"They won't," Vandar said with quiet conviction.

Yotra exhaled heavily, the weight of his decision lifting. "Then I'm sorry. I won't follow you anymore."

Vandar gave a small nod. "Thank you."

"Very touching," came a venomous voice behind them.

Both men turned to see Memphys pushing the girl forward, a knife pressed against her throat. Her other hand held a pistol aimed squarely at Vandar.

"Hands up," she barked. "Both of you."

Vandar raised his hands calmly. Yotra, after a moment's hesitation, followed suit.

Memphys's gaze burned with contempt as she spat at Vandar's feet. "Vandar Manak. The bastard who ruined everything. Drop your weapons."

Vandar removed his pistol and tossed it into the water. Memphys shifted her focus to Yotra.

"And you? Where's your gun?"

"I lost it," Yotra replied tersely.

"You useless idiot," she snapped. Her attention swung back to Vandar. "Where's Gravatis?"

Vandar's eyes flicked to the girl. "Don't hurt her, and you can have whatever you want."

Memphys sneered. "You expect me to trust you? I know your file, Manak. Ex-Kaldrosdom soldier, deadly at close range. I'm not getting anywhere near you."

She gestured at Yotra with her pistol. "You—fetch Gravatis."

Yotra stepped cautiously toward Vandar, who held the device in one hand. As he approached, Vandar tossed Gravatis into the air with a wink.

Memphys screamed as the device arced toward the waterfall's edge. She ran forward, slipping on the slick rocks, but Gravatis tumbled over the edge and disappeared into the churning water below.

"You bastard!" she shrieked, turning to fire at Vandar. But he moved swiftly, disarming her with a well-placed kick. The pistol flew over the edge, lost like Gravatis.

Memphys sank to her knees at the water's edge, staring helplessly into the white spray of the falls. Tears streamed down her face.

"It's over," Vandar said softly.

He retrieved his pistol, took the girl's hand, and began to walk away. Yotra watched as Memphys sobbed, her body trembling with defeat.

Vandar passed him, pausing briefly. "You should go while you can."

Yotra nodded, and they parted ways, leaving Memphys alone to mourn the loss of her mission—and her future with the Kaldrosdom.

36

The signal of Gravatis had stopped. It was destroyed in its fall into the waters. Memphys tucked the receiver away and stood in the clearing, adrift and purposeless. The fugitive was gone. Yotra Peak was gone. The girl was gone. She was utterly alone. With nothing else to cling to, she decided to climb down the rocky slope alongside the waterfall to the pool below. She would reclaim her pistol; it would still function after water exposure.

Her descent was slow and arduous, the jagged rocks tearing at her boots and damp uniform. When she reached the pool, its frigid water lapped at her ankles, then engulfed her as she dove into the icy depths. Searching through the blurry cold water, she dived again and again, her body numbed by the freezing currents. Hours passed.

Finally, she found the weapon lying among the grey and blue pebbles at the pool's bottom. Her fingers closed around its familiar shape. Clutching it tightly, she surfaced with a gasp, her limbs shaking uncontrollably. She dragged herself onto the shore, her teeth chattering as she lay sprawled on the rough bank, the setting sun casting long shadows over the valley.

Memphys looked at the pistol in her trembling hands, water dripping from its edges. She was exhausted, shivering uncontrollably in the evening breeze. The shadows of the cliffs grew longer, swallowing the dusty road she had taken into the mountains. Her gaze drifted toward the communicator in her belt. It blinked with a silent message. She pulled it out, her fingers clumsy and shaking.

The screen flashed:

"GRAVATIS SIGNAL LOST."

She froze. The words burned into her mind as the final confirmation of her failure. The receiver slipped from her fingers and landed in the dust with a dull thud. Memphys dropped to her knees, her soaked boots sinking into the earth. Her bloodied hair fell over her face as a sob escaped her lips. She buried her face in her hands and wept.

This was it. She had lost everything. Gravatis was gone, the fugitive untraceable, and the ship irretrievably stranded. Her failure was complete, and there would be no forgiveness from the Kaldros—or from Ilores.

She sat there for what felt like hours, the wind chilling her soaked body. Her bruised and aching hands found the pistol in her lap. She stared at it, her fingers tracing its edges as if searching for answers in its cold, unyielding metal. Slowly, deliberately, she raised it to her temple.

The pistol's metallic weight pressed against her skin. Tears streamed down her cheeks as she whispered to herself, "Forgive me."

The shot rang out, echoing through the valley and off the stone cliffs. Birds scattered into the dimming sky. Her body slumped to the ground, the pistol falling beside her. Blood pooled around her, dark and warm against the dusty road.

As her breath faded, Memphys found no peace. She would never know she was free—free from the Kaldrosdom, the Guild of Saturn, and the shadow of the Kaldros's merciless rule.

37

The pine trees loomed tall around them, their shadows lengthening as the sun dipped lower in the sky. Vandar and Theresa walked silently along the forest path, the fading roar of the waterfall giving way to the rustling of leaves and the occasional call of a bird. Theresa shivered as the air cooled, her arms crossed tightly over her chest. Vandar noticed and draped an arm over her shoulders, a gesture of warmth rather than intimacy. She didn't flinch, leaning slightly into him as they continued down the trail.

She had spoken little since the chaos at the waterfall. Vandar could see she was still processing what had happened, her confusion evident in her downcast eyes and hesitant steps. Though they had exchanged only a few words, he understood that their shared experience had forged a fragile connection. They walked on, the forest wrapping them in its quiet embrace.

Eventually, the path led to a ridge overlooking the valley below. Vandar stepped ahead, scanning the scene. Fields stretched from the base of the hills, a winding river cutting through the landscape like a glinting thread. A small village lay nestled near the valley's edge, its distant lights flickering as the evening approached. Vandar judged the distance and the encroaching shadows. They wouldn't make it before nightfall.

He turned to Theresa. "We should stay here," he said.

Her brows furrowed as she processed his unfamiliar accent. "Stay here?" she repeated carefully, her tone questioning.

"Yes," he confirmed, gesturing to the clearing. "I'll make a fire."

She hesitated, then nodded. Kneeling, she began gathering sticks, miming the act of striking a flame. Vandar chuckled softly, nodding his approval.

"I am Vandar," he said, watching her.

She straightened, holding the bundle of wood to her chest. "My name is Theresa."

"Theresa," he repeated, smiling. He found himself lingering on her name, the way it rolled off his tongue. Her sharp features and warm brown eyes captivated him, a beauty softened by the flickering shadows of the setting sun.

Pushing the thought aside, he focused on starting the fire. By the time night fell, they had built a crackling blaze, its warmth driving away the evening chill. The firelight danced across Theresa's face as she sat close, her arms wrapped around her knees.

"You are lucky I speak English," she said, her voice breaking the silence. She smiled, a hint of mischief in her eyes.

Vandar smiled back. "What other languages do you speak?"

She laughed lightly, shaking her head. "Italian, of course. You are in Italy, after all."

"I am?" Vandar asked, genuinely surprised.

Her laughter deepened, but as she studied him, her amusement gave way to curiosity. "You're serious?" she asked, tilting her head. "You didn't know?"

He shook his head, feeling uncharacteristically self-conscious. She leaned closer, her gaze dropping to his wrist. Her fingers brushed against the silver band he wore, tracing the alien engravings etched into its surface. She ran her hand over the fabric of his jacket, noticing its unusual texture.

"This is still wet," she said, tugging at his jacket. "It needs to dry."

Vandar helped her remove it, pulling his shirt off as well. The firelight caught the ridges of his chest, scars visible beneath his taut, bronzed skin. Theresa's eyes lingered on the marks, her fingers trailing over them.

"You've seen much," she murmured, her touch soft but deliberate.

Vandar's breath hitched as her lips moved closer to his. He

hesitated, unsure if he should pull back, but her warmth and presence were irresistible. When their lips met, the world seemed to fade, leaving only the fire's glow and the sound of their quiet breaths.

In that moment, Vandar let himself forget everything—the Kaldrosdom, Gravatis, and the pursuit that had brought him to this time. All that mattered was the woman before him and the connection they shared.

38

PART III
THE FALL OF THE TIME GATES

Shania soon learned that life went on beyond Richard Brooks. The New Year came, and she and her father were forgotten, their existence wiped clean by the activation of the Time Gates. She returned to school as a "new" pupil, and no one recognized her—because they didn't. Starting from scratch had its challenges, but it also came with advantages. Mistakes with friends were erased, leaving her free to rebuild relationships. Yet, she had to tread carefully, concealing her prior knowledge of others' lives to avoid suspicion or awkward questions.

Meeting Richard Brooks again, under fresh circumstances, turned out to be unexpectedly enjoyable. She could refine the process this time, avoiding old missteps and finding new ways to connect.

Her bond with her father deepened. They had always been close, but now they understood their shared reality: the only two of their kind in the world. Shania grew fascinated by her father's quiet strength. Beneath his simple, unassuming demeanor lay a man shaped by a violent, chaotic past. She would watch him tending the garden or picking her up from school in the Rover, marveling at how someone who had endured so much could appear so calm.

But the stories he had told her—his years of service to the

Kaldrosdom, the lives he had taken—haunted her. At night, she often heard his moans and cries, remnants of a world he had left behind but couldn't escape. She encouraged him to talk, though the sadness in his eyes when he did often left her wishing she hadn't asked. She wanted to heal him somehow, to find a way to reconcile him with the past he couldn't undo.

Yet, that same past was their shield against danger. The skills he had honed in the Kaldrosdom's service were now their greatest protection. They both lived with the lingering fear of Memphys Crowley's return, a specter of the night Shania's mother had been lost. Vandar, determined to prepare her, taught Shania the martial arts of the Kaldrosdom. She learned not just to fight, but to balance body and mind.

On the summit of Beacon Hill, the sun cast long shadows over the grassy expanse. Shania stood in a ready stance, her saber in hand and her fencing helmet on. Vandar inspected his own blade, running a finger along its edge. Though blunt, the occasional dent in the metal spoke of their many training sessions.

"Remember, technique and speed," he said. "This isn't about the force of the blow."

Shania nodded, lowering into a crouch to prepare for the bout. Vandar slipped on his helmet, mirroring her stance.

"Fight!" he barked.

The clash of metal echoed across the hilltop as their blades met. Their movements were swift and precise, feet shuffling in a dance of attack and defense. Shania deflected Vandar' strikes with calm efficiency, even managing a few well-timed counterattacks. Her confidence grew with every parry, her reflexes sharper than ever.

Vandar pressed forward, launching a rapid combination of high and low strikes. Shania stayed focused, her blade moving with practiced precision—until his saber feinted high. She panicked, swinging wildly to block the blow. Vandar' blade dipped beneath her wrist, coming to rest against her chest above her heart.

She froze, panting, the sound of their breathing filling the quiet space between them. Defeated, she removed her mask and wiped the sweat from her brow, her expression a mix of frustration and disappointment.

"You're progressing," Vandar said, lowering his blade. "You have stamina of the body, but not yet of the mind."

Shania lowered her gaze, ashamed of her mistake. Vandar stepped closer, placing a reassuring hand on her shoulder.

"You're already a better fighter than most at your level of training. You should be proud."

Her lips twitched into a small smile. "If you believe that, then I'm honored."

Vandar grinned and ruffled her hair playfully, knowing she hated it.

"You're wicked!" she laughed, shoving his hand away.

As the sun dipped lower, their laughter mingled with the gentle rustle of the breeze through the grass. For a moment, Beacon Hill felt like a world apart from the shadows of their past.

39

The drive through the hills of Tuscany was mesmerizing. Shania watched the fields rush past the car window, the rows of crumbling stone walls, endless plantations of olive trees, and small villas perched atop hilltops. She thought of this place, her mother's homeland, and smiled faintly. It felt surreal to finally return, even though the threat of Memphys Crowley still lingered in the shadows of their past. Somewhere in this country, her father's spaceship had crashed, forever tying their fates to this land. The car wound its way through the slopes toward the ancient fortress town of Arezzo, each turn bringing them closer to the moment her father had been dreading—and yearning for.

Vandar stood alone in the ancient piazza, his mind swirling with memories. The houses on the other side of the square loomed before him, their faded blue shutters watching over the cobblestones like sentinels of the past. His eyes settled on one particular window in the middle of the row. That had been his room, long ago. He lowered his gaze to the stones beneath his feet, his hands trembling at his sides.

From across the piazza, Shania approached, her soft footsteps barely audible. She had been walking alone through the town to give her father some space, but now she saw the weight of his thoughts etched across his face. She placed a comforting hand on his shoulder.

"I'm glad you're back," Vandar said, his voice heavy with emotion. He gestured toward the blue-shuttered window. "There. In the middle. That was my home."

Shania followed his gaze. The villa stood proud yet weathered, overlooking the square with quiet dignity.

"She's there now," Shania said gently. "I saw her in the market earlier. I followed her back to that house."

Vandar' breath caught in his throat. "This house?" he whispered, glancing at the familiar building.

Shania nodded. "It's the residence of Gino Forlanini. Your father-in-law still lives there."

Vandar closed his eyes, the weight of her words settling over him. He felt both relief and anguish. The past was no longer a memory—it was alive, breathing, waiting.

"Are you sure you want to do this?" Shania asked. She understood her father's need to face this moment, to confront the ghost of the life he'd lost. Yet it pained her to see him so vulnerable, so haunted.

"Yes," Vandar said firmly, though his voice wavered. "I must."

He squeezed her hand, drawing strength from her presence. Then, with a final glance at his daughter, he began crossing the piazza.

"I'll be here, waiting for you," Shania called after him. He turned briefly, offering her a sad smile.

"I love you," she added softly.

Vandar nodded, his eyes shimmering with unspoken gratitude, before continuing toward the villa.

The door was the same as he remembered: sturdy, weathered wood with a heavy brass knocker. Vandar hesitated, his hand hovering over the knocker. His heart pounded in his chest, each beat echoing the years of longing that had brought him to this moment. He closed his eyes, summoning the courage to face her, then knocked three times.

The pause that followed felt eternal. Then, the door creaked open, and there she was.

Theresa.

She was older, as he was, but her beauty had not faded. Her dark eyes were as deep and warm as he remembered, her face framed by the same dark waves of hair. Vandar' breath caught, his chest tightening as he struggled to find words.

"Si?" she asked, her voice soft and unfamiliar, yet achingly familiar all at once.

Vandar stared, tears welling in his eyes. He longed to hold her, to tell her everything. But she didn't recognize him. The realization hit him like a blow.

"Ti conosco?" Theresa asked, her brow furrowing.

"It's me," Vandar said, his voice breaking. "Vandar."

Theresa tilted her head, studying him. There was something in his voice that stirred a faint memory, like the echo of a dream. She stepped out from behind the door, closer to him, her expression a mixture of curiosity and compassion.

"I'm sorry," she said gently. "I don't think we've met."

Vandar' heart shattered, but he tried to smile. "We met on a train from Cinque Terre," he said, his words trembling. "You worked at a trattoria in Monterosso. You helped me when I was lost."

Theresa's eyes widened slightly. "I worked in Monterosso, yes. But I don't recall meeting you."

Vandar' shoulders sagged. He reached for one last thread of hope. "Shania," he said softly. "Does the name Shania mean anything to you?"

Theresa shook her head, confusion clouding her face. "I'm sorry," she said again. "I wish I could help you."

Her words cut through him like a blade. Vandar' knees buckled, and he reached for the doorframe to steady himself. Theresa's expression softened, and she stepped closer, placing a hand on his arm.

"I'm sorry," she said again, her voice filled with genuine empathy. "I can see you've lost someone. Someone you loved deeply."

Vandar couldn't hold back the tears any longer. He wept openly, and to his surprise, Theresa embraced him. For a brief, fleeting moment, it felt like old times—like he had returned to the life he had lost.

But then the moment ended. Theresa released him, stepping back toward the doorway.

"I'm sorry," she said one last time, her voice heavy with sadness. "But I don't know you."

She closed the door slowly, leaving Vandar alone in the piazza. He stood there for a long time, staring at the closed door, until the weight of his grief finally drove him to his knees.

40

The hotel room was white and sparsely furnished. The evening sky darkened, but the air remained warm and humid. Shania pulled the curtains shut and glanced over at her father, who had finally fallen asleep on the sofa. Hours of crying had left him curled up and silent. She watched his chest rise and fall with each breath.

"You sleep now," she whispered. "Dream of a better world."

She walked down the corridor toward the kitchen and noticed something glinting on the polished floorboards. It was silver, gleaming faintly in the dim light. She recognized it immediately—her father's wristband. He never took it off. For the first time, she held it in her hands, marveling at its weight and craftsmanship. The intricate patterns and alien symbols etched into the metal glowed faintly, pulsing in rhythm as if reacting to her touch.

She hesitated, tempted to try it on. Her father often meditated with it, lost in its mysteries, and she wondered what secrets it might reveal. She raised it above her wrist, ready to snap it into place, but paused. It was his, and she wouldn't disrespect that bond. Instead, she returned to his room and placed it gently in his hand. He stirred slightly, clutching it instinctively to his chest.

"What are you dreaming of, Father?" she whispered, brushing the sweat from his brow. She watched him for a moment, his face twitching with emotions she couldn't fathom, then left the room quietly.

He knew he was dreaming, but that didn't soften the horror. He stood atop a smoldering hill, surrounded by destruction. Flames licked at his boots, and the ground beneath was scorched black. Ash floated in the orange sky, heavy with smoke. Below, a valley stretched out, filled with people—men, women, children—fleeing in terror toward a distant town at the valley's base.

Then they appeared.

Emerging from the haze, the Carnos descended like vengeful specters. Cloaked in capes that billowed like smoke, they hovered effortlessly, their hands commanding fiery orbs that rained death on the helpless crowd. Screams ripped through the air as entire families were consumed in blinding flashes. The Carnos moved with deadly precision, recalling their weapons only to hurl them again, leaving nothing but devastation in their wake.

"No!" Vandar screamed, running down the hill, desperate to stop the slaughter. His legs burned, his lungs choked with smoke, but he didn't care. He wouldn't stop—not until the Carnos did. But they were too far, soaring beyond his reach. He fell to his knees, coughing, his fists pounding the ashen ground.

And then he saw her.

On a distant hill, silhouetted against the fiery sky, stood Shania. Dressed in white, her slender form glowed with an ethereal light. She raised her arms slowly, spreading them wide like wings. Vandar's heart froze as he realized her intention.

"Shania!" he shouted, his voice raw with panic. "Stop!"

She didn't hear him—or if she did, she didn't listen. Her wrist glinted with the silver bracelet of Tralonu ek Busca, its symbols shimmering like a beacon. With a grace that defied logic, she leapt into the air, soaring above the chaos below. Vandar watched, awestruck, as she glided effortlessly, a wingless angel cutting through the fiery sky.

Below her, the Carnos faltered. One by one, they tumbled from the heavens, their bodies crashing into the scorched earth like discarded marionettes. Their fiery orbs dimmed and fizzled, powerless without their masters. Vandar staggered forward, watching her ascend higher, her white form shrinking against the burning expanse.

"Shania!" he called again, his voice trembling with a mixture of fear and awe.

She didn't look back. Her form disappeared into the horizon, leaving him alone in the inferno. The smoldering world faded around him, the ash and fire dissolving into darkness.

Vandar woke with a gasp, his chest heaving as if he'd been suffocating. He clutched the wristband tightly against his chest, its metallic surface cool against his skin. Beads of sweat rolled down his face, and his pulse thundered in his ears.

In the next room, Shania stirred at the sound, but she didn't return to him. She sat silently in the kitchen, staring at the empty space before her, sensing the weight of her father's dreams pressing through the walls.

41

Vandar sat on the bench on the villa's veranda, gazing out at the golden afternoon. The air was warm, the hum of distant life faint but steady. Shania's laughter drifted up the driveway as she cycled with Richard, her carefree joy a contrast to the weight he carried. He watched her stop at the gate, talking animatedly to the boy before waving him off. She wheeled her bicycle onto the lawn and climbed the steps.

"Good afternoon," she said, smiling. "You never sit out here."

"That's an exaggeration," Vandar replied, grinning.

"You know it's true," she teased, sitting beside him. "You hate sitting still."

Vandar chuckled, conceding. "Fine. I rarely sit here."

Her laughter faded as she noticed the contemplative look in his eyes. "Are you okay?"

He took a deep breath, then removed the bracelet from his wrist. Its silver surface gleamed in the sunlight, the intricate symbols and markings catching the light as though alive.

"I want you to have this," he said, placing it in her hands.

Her wide eyes darted between him and the bracelet. "I... I couldn't."

"Yes, you can," he said, closing her hands around it with his own. "It belongs with you now."

"But... why?" she asked, her voice trembling. "You've always worn it—it's always been yours."

Vandar smiled faintly. "It was never truly mine. This bracelet belongs to Tralonu ek Busca. It's his legacy, his story... and now it's yours."

Shania studied the bracelet, its surface impossibly smooth, the etched symbols pulsating faintly as if sensing her touch. A strange warmth coursed through her fingers.

"Who was Tralonu ek Busca?" she asked softly.

Vandar leaned back, his gaze distant. "He was a traveler, a being older than any human can comprehend. He came to the Kingdom during Kaldrosdom David's reign, long before the darkness that followed. Tralonu ek Busca brought wisdom, warning, and knowledge of the universe. But he also carried secrets—secrets that humanity, in its greed, wasn't ready for."

Vandar paused, gathering his thoughts, and began the tale of Tralonu ek Busca.

"Kaldrosdom David's Kingdom was small and peaceful, a shining beacon in a newly settled world. One day, soldiers discovered a lone spaceship adrift in space. Inside was Tralonu ek Busca—a being of impossible age and frailty. He was brought to the Guild of Saturn, where the Kaldrosdom himself welcomed him. David, pure of heart, ordered his best scientist, Ilores, to care for Tralonu and learn from him.

"Tralonu shared wonders beyond imagination: tales of galaxies, the balance of time and space, and a map of Horus, a black hole so massive it seemed alive, prowling the edges of the Milky Way. His knowledge saved countless lives, warning of cosmic dangers humanity could not yet comprehend. But when it came to the mysteries of his longevity and advanced technology, Tralonu was guarded. He feared what humanity might do with such power."

Shania listened intently, her fingers tracing the bracelet's symbols. "What happened?"

"Ilores grew impatient. He respected Tralonu but couldn't ignore the temptation of his secrets. Time passed, and Kaldrosdom David grew older. Fearing the rise of his cruel son, Fortame, David confided in Ilores. And Ilores—ambitious, cunning—offered the Kaldrosdom a solution: immortality."

Vandar's voice hardened. "David resisted at first, but doubt crept in. When an accident left Ilores near death, Tralonu took him to his ship to save him. Ilores, feigning gratitude, awoke with the knowledge he craved. He betrayed Tralonu, imprisoning him in darkness to extract his secrets."

Shania's eyes filled with tears. "That's awful. Did Tralonu escape?"

Vandar shook his head. "He endured centuries of torment, refusing to reveal the location of his home or his final truths. Before he died, he crafted this bracelet, embedding it with his wisdom and legacy. It was lost for generations until it came to me."

Shania looked at the bracelet, her heart heavy. "And now it's mine?"

Vandar nodded. "You carry his story, his wisdom, and his hope for a better future. You'll know when to use it. Trust yourself."

She looked at him, her voice trembling. "I don't know if I'm ready."

"You are," Vandar said, his voice steady. "You're stronger than you know."

She held the bracelet close, its warmth comforting. "I'll honor him, and you. I promise."

Vandar smiled, his eyes misty. "That's all I could ask for."

The sun dipped lower, casting golden light over them as Shania embraced her father, the weight of her new responsibility settling on her shoulders—and her heart.

42

Shania sprinted over the grassy slopes of Beacon Hill, the winter air biting at her lungs. Her breath formed small clouds as she pushed herself harder, charging across ridges and down ditches carved into the hill's summit. The cold barely registered; her focused mind and relentless pace kept her warm.

Over the past three years, her visions had become more vivid, powerful, and impossible to ignore. The bracelet had shown her distant galaxies and Tranlonu ek Busca's incredible journeys. At first, these visions came fleetingly in dreams or meditations. But now they were stronger, often accompanied by intense emotions that lingered long after they ended.

She had seen horrors that haunted her waking moments: the **Time Gates**, massive constructs of jagged crescents spinning around a central globe, floating ominously in a barren part of space. She'd felt Ilores' malevolence and witnessed the Kaldros, a soulless tyrant whose gaze seemed to pierce directly into her own through the visions, threatening to drag her into his darkness.

The universe called out for justice. And she felt its weight upon her shoulders.

Reaching the summit of Beacon Hill for the third time that day, she paused, hands on her hips, her breath steadying. She scanned the patchwork fields below, neatly divided by hedgerows, with Highclere Castle rising stoically in the distance.

"The time has come," she murmured, her voice firm.

Vandar lay under the truck, tightening bolts on the engine when he heard footsteps crunching on the gravel driveway. He paused, listening.

"Who's there?" he called, sliding out on his wheeled service trolley.

He spotted boots approaching—boots he recognized. It was Shania. But as she came into view, he saw someone different. She was no longer a child; she was a woman now—twenty years old, tall, athletic, and exuding an unshakable resolve. Her serious expression told him everything before she even spoke.

"You need to take me back to your ship," she said.

Vandar blinked, confused, as he wiped his hands on a cloth. "My ship?"

She nodded. "The one that crashed in the sea near Cinque Terre. We must return to it."

Recognition flickered in his eyes. He stood, studying her. Gone was the soft, carefree Shania of his memories. This woman carried the weight of something greater, something beyond herself. Though he had known this day would come, he couldn't help but feel a pang of sadness for the innocence she had left behind.

"We'll make preparations," he said with a nod.

She didn't hesitate. "Never mind the truck. I'll buy us a four-wheel drive."

She turned and strode toward the house without another word, leaving Vandar standing by the old vehicle.

He sighed heavily, running a hand over the hood. "Well, old girl, looks like you're over the hill, just like me."

He tossed the tools onto the seat inside and followed Shania into the house, knowing she wouldn't wait long before wanting to leave.

43

The stormy northern Italian coastline stretched before them, a vast expanse of churning waves crashing against the rocky shore. Shania stood on the sand beside her father, bundled in a waterproof jacket but still feeling the bite of the autumn winds. Vandar scanned the horizon, his face lined with concentration as he held a pair of binoculars to his eyes.

"It's here," Vandar muttered, lowering the binoculars. His eyes darted to the waves lapping against the shore and the odd stillness just beyond the breaking surf.

Shania turned to him. "How can you tell? It's invisible."

Vandar crouched down, running his fingers through the damp sand. "You can't hide something this big, even with a cloaking shield," he explained. "Look at the water." He pointed toward a strange eddy swirling unnaturally close to the shore, where no current should be.

"And the fish," he continued, nodding toward the tide pools nearby. "See how there aren't any? That's not normal. The ship's shields disrupt the natural magnetic fields—marine life avoids it."

Shania tilted her head, examining the water with newfound curiosity. The ripples Vandar had pointed out seemed subtle at first, but once she saw them, she couldn't unsee the eerie stillness in the ocean's rhythm.

"So, what's the plan?" she asked.

Vandar grinned, the kind of mischievous smile she'd come to

associate with his more daring ideas. "I'll use some markers to confirm the ship's position. It won't be exact, but it'll give us a sense of where to swim."

He reached into his backpack, pulling out a handful of brightly colored, lightweight balls that floated on the surface of the water. "These should catch on the hull if we toss them out far enough."

Shania raised an eyebrow. "That's it?"

"No," Vandar admitted. "There's more to it than this. But these markers will give us an idea of the edges. After that..." He hesitated, looking at her seriously. "I'm relying on you."

"Me?" Shania asked, taken aback.

"You've seen things I can't even imagine," Vandar said. "The bracelet connects you to patterns I've only glimpsed. If anyone can pinpoint the ship, it's you."

She nodded, the weight of his words settling over her. "Alright. Let's do this."

Vandar started by tossing the floating markers into the surf. The wind whipped at his hair as he watched the tiny balls bounce and drift on the surface. At first, they scattered randomly, but after several tosses, some of them began to clump together inexplicably, forming a loose curve in the water.

"That's it," Vandar murmured, pointing to the irregular line. "The edge of the ship. The cloaking shield is pushing the water slightly, creating that pattern."

Shania stared at the area, her heart pounding. "And you're sure it's stable? The shield isn't... dangerous?"

"It shouldn't be," Vandar said, though his voice carried a note of uncertainty. "But we'll find out soon enough."

Shania closed her eyes, gripping the bracelet on her wrist. She let the chaotic sounds of the wind and waves fade into the background, focusing instead on the faint hum she felt deep within. A pulse, almost imperceptible, seemed to call out from the ocean.

"There," she whispered, pointing beyond the markers. "I can feel it. The ship's energy—it's drawing the water toward it, subtly but steadily."

Vandar gave her an encouraging smile. "Good. Now we swim."

The icy waves crashed against them as they waded into the sea, their movements slow and deliberate against the strong currents. Shania kept her focus on the sensation in her mind, like a thread leading her through the dark. Vandar swam beside her, his face set with determination.

After what felt like an eternity, Vandar stopped abruptly. His hand hit something solid, though nothing was visible.

"Here!" he called over the roar of the waves. "The hull!"

He slapped the invisible surface with his palm, feeling its cold, barnacle-covered exterior. Shania reached out, her fingers brushing against the same unseen wall.

Vandar laughed, a sound of both triumph and relief. "We found it!"

Shania smiled despite the cold. "Now what?"

"There should be a ladder leading up," Vandar said. He ran his hands along the surface, searching blindly. "Got it!"

As Vandar climbed, the rain lashed against them, making the invisible ladder slippery. Shania followed close behind, her senses still attuned to the ship's presence. Halfway up, a sudden surge of energy rippled through her—like the ship was responding to her.

The hull shimmered faintly, and for a brief moment, the ship's massive form became visible against the stormy sky.

Vandar glanced back, wide-eyed. "What did you do?"

"I... don't know," Shania admitted, gripping the ladder tightly. "It's like the ship knows I'm here."

They reached the top, and as they stepped onto the invisible deck, an airlock door hissed open. Bright light spilled out, illuminating the rain-soaked metal.. He froze.

The line widened, glowing so brightly that Vandar shielded his eyes. As his vision adjusted, he saw her—a figure stepping out of the light.

Memphys Crowley.

Dressed in her Kingdom uniform, she strode onto the deck with chilling confidence, her hand hovering near her holstered pistol. "What a surprise," she sneered.

Vandar drew his weapon, lowering his center of gravity against the ship's slippery surface. The wind howled around them.

Memphys smirked, removing her hand from the pistol. "I've waited years for this. Let's settle it." She lunged, closing the distance in a blur. Vandar fired, but she rolled across the deck, evading the blasts. The ship shimmered briefly as the camouflage flickered, disorienting him. Before he could react, Memphys was upon him, delivering a sharp kick that sent his pistol skidding over the edge into the sea.

Shania reached the deck just as Memphys gained the upper hand. Vandar collapsed under a barrage of punches, struggling to defend himself. When Memphys drew her blade, Shania screamed, charging forward. Memphys turned, redirecting her aim toward the oncoming girl. Shania dove under the shot, sliding across the deck before springing to her feet. She tackled Memphys, the two women grappling fiercely.

"You'll die just like your mother!" Memphys hissed, twisting Shania's arm. Shania cried out but retaliated with a brutal headbutt, sending Memphys reeling.

Memphys staggered, wiping blood from her nose. "You're tougher than you look," she snarled. "But it won't save you."

She lashed out, landing a powerful kick that sent Shania sliding toward the ship's edge. Clinging desperately to a seam in the hull, Shania watched helplessly as Memphys stood over Vandar, blade poised for the kill.

"Any last words, Manak?" Memphys taunted.

Vandar didn't respond, his body limp.

Shania's despair gave way to something deeper. The wristband on her arm began to glow, its alien symbols pulsating with light. The ship rumbled, rocking violently. Memphys faltered, her balance shifting.

"What the hell?" Memphys shouted, looking around. She raised the knife again, but Shania moved—no, flew.

Shania's body became weightless, propelled forward as if by an unseen force. Her face was calm, her movements deliberate. Memphys' knife froze mid-air, held in place by the same invisible power.

"What is this?!" Memphys screamed, turning to face her attacker.

Shania stretched out her hand. The knife spun, reversing direction, and shot back toward Memphys with lethal speed. Memphys barely had time to react before the blade buried itself in her chest. She staggered, her eyes wide with shock, before collapsing backward. Her body slid across the deck and disappeared into the stormy sea below.

Shania landed softly, her feet steady on the ship's deck. Ignoring the chaos around her, she rushed to her father's side. Vandar was unconscious but breathing. She dragged him into the airlock, her heart pounding as the door sealed shut.

Outside, the ship's shimmering form disappeared, blending once more into the raging ocean, leaving no trace of the battle that had unfolded.

44

Vandar stirred awake, his head pounding and his body aching. The rhythmic tapping of rain on metal reached his ears, and he slowly opened his eyes. He was sitting in a padded chair, still drenched in his soaking wet uniform. As his vision cleared, he realized the air around him was warmer and calm, a stark contrast to the chaos he last remembered.

He blinked hard, his mind catching up to his surroundings. Before him stood Shania, her silhouette framed by a viewing screen displaying a stormy, rain-soaked sea. The rolling grey clouds outside cast her in a muted glow. She stood still, her back to him, gazing into the tempest as if seeing far beyond the horizon.

Vandar' gaze shifted to the chair he was in, and recognition jolted through him.

"The ship," he whispered, his voice filled with disbelief.

The seat, the consoles, the distinct layout—it was the cockpit of the ship that had carried him to Earth over two decades ago. The memories flooded back: his desperate escape from the Kingdom, the anguish of leaving everything behind, and the fragile hope of a new beginning. Now, here he was, back in the heart of it all.

Shania turned, noticing his movement. A soft smile crossed her lips as she walked to him.

"Father," she said gently, her voice carrying a mix of relief and affection.

He reached for her, pulling her into a tight embrace.

"I thought I'd lost you," she murmured.

"Lose me?" he teased, his voice rough but warm. "You should be so lucky."

She laughed softly, a sound that lightened the weight in his chest. As she pulled back, Vandar studied her face, noting the change in her. She was no longer the carefree child he had raised but a woman filled with purpose.

"You've become… something incredible," he said, his voice tinged with awe.

Shania nodded, her expression solemn. "And so have you. But now, we must act."

Vandar looked past her to the viewing screen, the storm-wracked sea gradually shrinking as the ship rose. He stiffened. "We're… moving?"

She smiled faintly, her eyes distant as if listening to a voice he couldn't hear.

"Yes," she said simply. "The ship is taking us where we need to go."

Vandar frowned. "But Gravatis is gone. The ship can't—"

"Gravatis is no longer a machine," she interrupted, stepping back. "It's a force, and it lives within me."

His heart sank as her meaning hit him. "Shania, no—"

"This is my purpose, Father. The universe has shown me." She raised her arms slightly, and the bracelet of Tralonu ek Busca glowed faintly on her wrist. "We must confront the Kaldros, Ilores, and the Time Gates. There's no other way."

Vandar felt his stomach twist. The idea of willingly returning to the Kingdom—the place he had risked everything to escape—filled him with dread.

"How can we defeat them?" he asked, his voice barely a whisper.

"The same way we were guided here," she said, her voice unwavering. "By the balance of the universe itself."

The ship rumbled beneath them as it ascended, clouds swallowing them whole. Vandar stumbled slightly, catching himself on a console.

"Shania, you're putting yourself in danger. This is madness," he said, his tone pleading.

She turned to him, her eyes calm but resolute. "You've always taught me to fight for what's right, no matter the cost. Now it's my turn to lead."

Vandar wanted to argue, to protect her, but the determination in her gaze silenced him. He had always known this moment might come, but now that it had, he wasn't ready to let her go.

Outside, the ship burst through the thick clouds, the endless black of space revealing itself. Stars glittered like distant beacons, and the stormy world below faded into insignificance. Vandar gazed at the view, a mixture of wonder and dread filling his heart.

Shania staggered slightly, her body trembling as she lowered her arms. Vandar rushed to her side, steadying her.

"Are you alright?" he asked, his voice tight with worry.

She nodded, her breathing uneven. "I'm fine. Just… adjusting."

He helped her to a seat and knelt beside her. "Shania, you don't have to carry this alone."

She placed a hand on his arm, her touch both gentle and firm. "I'm not alone. We're in this together."

He looked into her eyes, seeing the same spark of determination that had carried him through his own trials. Slowly, he nodded.

"What's the plan?" he asked.

Her lips curved into a faint smile. "We strike at the next Quantisation. Midnight. That's when Ilores will be at the Time Gates."

Vandar' chest tightened. The Quantisation—New Year's Day—the point where time itself was reset. Returning to that moment meant returning to the heart of the Kingdom's power.

"How are we supposed to stop him?" he asked.

Shania's expression softened. "The same way you stopped running, Father. By facing what must be faced."

He sat back, the enormity of their task pressing down on him. But as he looked at his daughter, he felt a flicker of hope. If anyone could bring balance to the universe, it was her.

He stood and moved to the console, his hands moving across the controls with the ease of familiarity. "Alright," he said, glancing at her. "Let's save the universe."

Shania's smile widened, and for a moment, the weight of their mission felt lighter. Together, they turned their focus to the stars, ready to face whatever lay ahead.

45

The ship soared through space, its sleek frame cutting effortlessly through the void. After weeks of travel, they approached Jupiter, its colossal presence dominating the view. Shania stood at the viewport, awestruck by the planet's size and the swirling storms of its atmosphere.

Vandar manned the controls, guiding the ship into position. "This is it," he said. "Jupiter's gravity will give us the boost we need to achieve light speed."

Shania closed her eyes, reaching out with her mind. She felt the ship's pull toward Jupiter, the immense energy coursing through the cosmos. The patterns of the universe aligned in her consciousness, revealing the perfect trajectory.

As the ship slingshot around Jupiter, Shania channeled its gravity, redirecting its force to propel them forward. The vessel rumbled, the engines straining against the immense energy. Vandar gripped the controls tightly, his eyes flicking between the viewport and the monitors.

Flashes of light began to streak past the ship as they approached the threshold of light speed. Shania opened her eyes, her face serene.

"We've entered the stream," she said softly.

Vandar glanced at her, awed by her calm demeanor. "We're really doing this."

The ship shuddered violently as it broke through the light-speed barrier, the stars outside stretching into brilliant lines of light. Shania exhaled deeply, her connection to the cosmos steadying the ship's passage.

46

It was the thirty-first of January when they decelerated below light speed and emerged into the future. The vastness of the cosmos stretched before them, and not far ahead loomed the enigmatic Time Gates, their shimmering structures both mesmerizing and foreboding. They approached cautiously, the ship's sensors scanning every detail.

The monstrous black hole, Horus, loomed ominously in the distance, a cosmic predator edging closer to the Time Gates as it did with every cosmic cycle. Shania had skillfully manipulated Horus' immense gravitational pull to decelerate their craft, bringing them into the time of Vandar' origin—a precise, dangerous maneuver only she could execute.

Vandar leaned over his console, studying the intricate holographic display of the Time Gates.
"It will be heavily fortified," he said, his voice tinged with both respect and wariness. "The perimeter defenses are formidable. And inside..." He paused, glancing at Shania. "Carnos will be waiting."

Shania crossed her arms, her mind already working through the challenge.
"We'll need a way in," she said decisively. "A ruse to bypass their defenses."

Before Vandar could respond, a harsh alarm pierced the stillness of the cabin. The lights on the pilot's console flickered ominously. Shania's sharp gaze turned to Vandar as he moved swiftly to the controls and slid into the chair.

"What's happening?" she asked, her tone calm but edged with urgency.

Vandar' fingers danced over the console, his expression grim.

"We've got company," he said, his voice steady despite the tension in the air.

47

Prince Sorrell's ship dropped from light speed and slipped into the desolate flight path toward the Time Gates. The vast emptiness of space stretched endlessly before them, stars glinting faintly in the void. Sorrell sat rigid on the flight deck, his pale hands clenched over the armrests. Sleep had become a distant memory, stolen by the weight of betrayal and rebellion.

He would soon face his father. The thought churned in his stomach like a storm, an unrelenting reminder of the gravity of his actions. He glanced out the viewport, scanning the black expanse ahead. Somewhere, beyond this nothingness, lay the Time Gates—his father's crowning creation. Sorrell had never seen them before; his father's paranoia had kept them veiled in secrecy. But now, thanks to Ilores, he was here. A pawn invited to the game, ready to turn the board.

He would find the cracks in the armor. He had to.

"Your Highness," the pilot's voice broke the silence, low and urgent. "Unidentified spacecraft on approach."

Sorrell turned sharply, his dark eyes narrowing.
"Out here? That's impossible."

Before the pilot could respond, the ship shuddered violently. The lights dimmed, flickering erratically before plunging the flight deck into crimson shadows. A deep, mechanical groan echoed through the hull, followed by a resounding thud that made the deck plates vibrate beneath their feet.

"What the hell was that?" Sorrell demanded, his voice taut.

The pilot's fingers flew over the console, a sheen of sweat gleaming on his forehead. "Gravatis drive... it's failed."

"Failed?" Sorrell repeated, his voice colder now, razor-edged with disbelief. This ship was supposed to be beyond failure—untouchable. Yet here they were, stranded.

"My Prince!" the pilot shouted, jabbing a finger toward the viewport.

Sorrell turned, and his breath caught. The silhouette of a ship loomed ahead, closing in fast. Its lines were brutal and practical—a prison transport, yet it bristled with laser cannons that gleamed ominously in the red glow.

"They're hailing us," the pilot said, his voice cracking. "Demanding surrender."

Sorrell's jaw tightened as he stared at the vessel. His mind raced through options, none of them good. Their systems were crippled, and their ship hung like prey in a hunter's trap.

"They have us, sir. We're defenseless," the pilot added, his tone edged with panic.

A silence stretched, sharp and suffocating, before Sorrell exhaled slowly.
"Tell them we agree," he said, his voice calm but weighted with fury.

As the pilot relayed their surrender, Sorrell's mind churned. He hadn't come this far to fall here. The prison ship had them, but it wouldn't hold him for long.

48

The red emergency lights bathed the flight deck in an oppressive glow, casting jagged shadows across Prince Sorrell as he slumped in his chair, bound by his guard's handcuffs. He stared at the cold metal floor, his thoughts spiraling. How could this have happened? What force was powerful enough to cripple his entire ship?

The Gravatis drive was silent, and the backup circuits were dead. Only the faint hum of the air pumps kept the freezing void of space from overtaking them. Even so, the temperature was plummeting, the chill creeping into Sorrell's bones. He shivered and exhaled slowly, watching his breath condense in the dim light.

The scuffle had been brief. Sorrell hadn't seen it—he'd only heard the sickening sound of his guards being slammed into the walls. Then, she had appeared: a young woman in a Kingdom uniform, disarming and subduing him as if it were routine. Now, his crew was imprisoned in the brig, and he was left alone with his captors.

The pair were unusual. The man, scarred and rugged, had the air of a seasoned warrior, his calm gaze masking years of hardship. The woman, younger but far more unsettling, radiated an intensity that made Sorrell uneasy. Her presence stirred something primal—both a faint desire and an instinctive wariness.

"What do you want?" Sorrell asked, his voice cold but faltering slightly.

The man leaned casually against the console, his dark eyes

meeting Sorrell's. "This ship—it's a royal transport. Just who are you?"

Sorrell's eyes narrowed. "Who are you to ask?" he shot back.

The man smirked, taking a slow step forward. "Vandar Manak," he said, his tone even. He nodded toward the woman. "And this is Shania, my daughter. Now, let's try again—who are you?"

Sorrell hesitated, weighing his options. These people had already subdued his entire crew. What choice did he have but to answer? He straightened slightly in his chair, his pride struggling against his predicament.

"I am Sorrell, son of the Kaldros," he said at last.

Vandar raised an eyebrow, his expression unreadable. Shania, however, let out a faint, knowing laugh.

"Prince Sorrell," Vandar repeated, his voice tinged with intrigue. "Truly?"

"What do you want with me?" Sorrell demanded, deflecting their scrutiny.

Vandar folded his arms. "We need access to the Time Gates."

Sorrell barked a bitter laugh. "You're insane. That place is the most heavily defended stronghold in the Kingdom. Do you have any idea what you're walking into?"

"Which is why we need your ship to get in," Shania said, her voice sharp and steady.

Sorrell's jaw tightened. "The Time Gates are the Kaldros's crown jewel. What you're planning is suicide!"

Vandar tilted his head, studying Sorrell. "You're the Kaldros's son. Why are you so afraid?"

Sorrell's gaze darkened, his voice dropping to a bitter whisper. "Because even I am not safe from my father's wrath. You have no idea what he's capable of. If you have any sense, you'll turn this ship around and disappear."

Shania's eyes narrowed. "It's because we have sense that we're ignoring you, Prince. Ilores must die, as must your tyrant father."

Sorrell stiffened, his anger rising. "You'll ruin everything! I'm building an army—I'm planning to challenge the Kaldros myself. Your recklessness puts all of it at risk!"

Vandar smiled faintly, leaning closer. "Then it's simple. When we arrive, you go about your business as planned. Disembark the ship, say nothing of us, and by the time you're finished, we'll be gone—undetected."

Sorrell studied Vandar, his mind racing. The man's scarred arms and the sword at his belt marked him as a warrior. Shania, however, was more difficult to place. Her intensity unsettled him; her saintly aura repelled him even as her presence sparked something deeper. He could not trust them, but their plan intrigued him.

"Very well," Sorrell said finally. "You have my word. Disappear from my ship at the first opportunity. Do not be detected."

Shania gave him a thin, cold smile. "Then we agree."

She closed her eyes, raising a hand. A low hum reverberated through the ship as the systems flickered back to life. The Gravatis drive roared, and the lights returned. Sorrell stared in stunned silence as the ship surged forward.

The Time Gates loomed ahead, monstrous and foreboding. Jagged crescents rose like skeletal talons around a glowing central sphere. Their ship was an insect compared to the towering structure, dwarfed by its grotesque grandeur.

"Look," Shania said, pointing beyond the Time Gates.

In the void beyond, a perfect circle of blackness devoured the light of distant stars.

"Horus," Shania whispered.

Sorrell squinted. "What is that?"

"A black hole of immense size," she replied. "It powers the Time Gates—and your father's grip on the universe."

Sorrell's chest tightened as the ship docked. The enormity of his father's creation struck him anew, leaving him pale and trembling. Vandar turned to him, his voice steady but firm.

"Remember—not a word about us."

Sorrell nodded weakly, his hands shaking. He rose unsteadily to his feet, glancing at the pair one last time.

"You have my word," he said.

As Sorrell stepped onto the gangway, Shania moved silently to her father's side. Her hand brushed his belt, slipping the sword free without a sound. This was her battle—not Vandar'.

From the viewport, Shania watched as a small party approached the ship. At their center stood Ilores, his silver form glinting under the lights, his purple robes flowing like liquid shadows. Shania's heart pounded, her hatred burning brighter than ever.

"Ilores approaches," she said softly.

Vandar frowned. "How can you be sure?"

Her eyes narrowed. "I've seen him before."

Sorrell, now halfway down the ramp, glanced back briefly before turning to Ilores. Bowing deeply, he greeted the man who embodied everything Shania sought to destroy.

49

Sorrell's heart pounded relentlessly as he walked alongside the silver man. Each step felt heavier, his chest constricting under the weight of his deception. Ilores, however, moved with calm precision. His metallic face betrayed no emotion, his movements unnervingly smooth.

"It is an honor to host you here at the Time Gates, Prince Sorrell," Ilores said, his voice resonant and mechanical. "You will soon witness the power and beauty of The Quantisation."

Sorrell stole a glance back toward his ship, now hidden from view. His breath hitched as he tried to steady himself. If luck was on his side, his betrayal would go unnoticed—at least for now.

"Thank you, Lord Ilores," he managed, his words carefully measured. "It is... humbling to witness the workings of my father's Kingdom. My only wish is to see it secure for all time."

Ilores gave no response, his gaze fixed ahead. They stopped at the edge of an enormous glass dome, its curved walls offering a panoramic view of the heavens. Ilores gestured grandly, his movements smooth but deliberate.

"Behold," Ilores intoned.

Sorrell's eyes were drawn upward. Beyond the dome's crystal-clear surface, the monstrous black hole Horus loomed. A void so vast and consuming, it devoured light itself. The stars around it twisted into surreal patterns, and the skeletal arms of the Time Gates stretched toward it like talons, poised to claw at its unspeakable power.

Sorrell gripped the platform's handrail, his knuckles white. The sight was overwhelming—an alien combination of beauty and horror. His chest tightened as panic clawed at the edges of his mind.

"How could anyone stop this?" The thought stabbed through him, a cruel reminder of his insignificance. The power he had once dreamed of wielding now seemed laughable.

Ilores raised his arms toward the void. "In three short hours," he said, his voice rising with reverence, "Horus will reach its closest point. The Time Gates will spin, harnessing its power to correct time —restoring the glory of the Kaldros to all centuries, even those ignorant of his reign."

Sorrell's stomach churned. The scale of their plan was staggering.

"Do you see now, Prince Sorrell," Ilores said, turning to face him, "the power your father and I wield?"

The silver man stepped closer, his metallic finger extending like a blade. Sorrell instinctively backed away, his breath hitching.

"And yet," Ilores hissed, his voice hardening, "you—a mere mortal —dare to think you can challenge the Kaldros? The Kaldros of a thousand years?"

Sorrell froze, his mind racing. Ilores' empty, glowing eyes bore into him like daggers.

"Yes," Ilores rasped, his tone sharper now. "I know of your pathetic 'army' on Jupiter—crushed. Your plan to give Gravatis to the Genowans? Exposed. You are a traitor, unworthy of the title 'Prince.'"

Ilores lunged, his silver hand clamping around Sorrell's throat with inhuman strength.

Sorrell's hands shot up, clawing at Ilores' grip, but the metallic fingers were unyielding. He tried to speak, to plead, to reveal the stowaways on his ship—his last chance for reprieve—but no sound escaped.

His lungs burned, his vision darkened, and the world spun wildly. The agony was unbearable, his blood thundering in his ears as his body convulsed.

Then, suddenly, a strange calm washed over him. A surge of chemicals dulled the pain and quieted his panic. His mind drifted, detached from the chaos.

Nothing mattered anymore.

He became a fragile boat, floating on a vast, indifferent sea. The wind could change, the waters could consume him, and it would mean nothing.

Ilores' silver face was the last thing Sorrell's failing eyes could hold onto, the final fragment of a world slipping away. Slowly, the edges of reality blurred, and the silver figure dissolved into darkness.

Sorrell's body went limp. Ilores released his grip, and the Prince crumpled to the floor like a broken doll, his head striking the platform with a hollow thud. His lifeless form sprawled at the silver man's feet, a pale shadow of defiance extinguished.

Ilores straightened, flexing his metallic fingers. Without a glance at the fallen Prince, he turned back toward the towering machinery of the Time Gates. The Quantisation awaited, and soon, the Kaldros's glory would span all of time.

50

Shania fastened her belt, securing her sword at her side. With a steadying breath, she opened the ship's door to the exit ramp. Her gaze swept across the hangar toward the gateway leading to the globe.

"We'll need to keep well hidden," she said, her voice low but firm. "This area is heavily guarded by the Carnos."

Vandar nodded, his usual confident grin on his face. He was ready —for battle, for sacrifice, for whatever was needed. As he reached for his sword, his fingers brushed against a different weight. He froze, his expression shifting to confusion.

"Wait!" he rasped, his voice rough with urgency. "My sword—it's gone!"

His eyes darted wildly around the cockpit, his mind racing. Then it hit him. "The Prince," he muttered, the pieces snapping together.

Turning sharply, he scanned the room. Relief surged through him as his gaze landed on the familiar sheath, tucked behind the co-pilot's seat. He crossed the room in long strides, reclaiming it with a sense of triumph.

But as he turned back toward the door, the triumph dissolved.

Shania stood framed in the open doorway, her sword belted at her side. Her face was heavy with sadness, her eyes lingering on him for a moment too long.

"Shania, no," he said, his voice cracking with desperate urgency.

"You need me."

"I'm sorry, Father," she whispered, her voice trembling.

Vandar lunged forward, his hand outstretched. "Don't —"

The door hissed shut with a sharp finality, cutting him off mid-sentence.

"Shania!" he roared, slamming his fists against the sealed door with a force that reverberated through the cockpit. His voice cracked, raw with panic, but the door remained unyielding.

Outside, a tear rolled down Shania's cheek. She opened her eyes, staring at the cold metal panel before her.

"Goodbye," she whispered.

The engines roared to life, the sound reverberating through the hangar. Shania stood motionless, her hands clenched at her sides. She had done what was necessary, though it left a hollow ache in her chest. As the ship disappeared into the tunnel and out into space, she whispered a silent prayer for her father's safety.

The hangar fell silent, the air heavy with finality. Shania stood alone, the weight of her decision pressing down on her like the cold metal walls around her. There was no turning back now.

51

He yelled for her to stop, but it was too late. The door sealed with a sharp hiss, and the ship's engines roared to life. Vandar sprinted to the door, hammering on the controls frantically, but they didn't respond. The ship was no longer his—it was hers now, moving to Shania's will.

He felt the vessel lurch as it backed away from the platform, then pivot sharply toward the exit tunnel. Panic surged through him, and he stumbled to the nearest window, pressing his trembling hands against the cold glass.

Through blurred vision, he saw her. Shania stood motionless on the platform's edge, her eyes closed, her face calm yet resolute. She was guiding the ship with her thoughts, her figure framed by the vast expanse of the hangar behind her.

Vandar' chest tightened as he watched her retreat further into the distance, her figure shrinking with every passing second. He pressed his palm flat against the glass, as if trying to reach her through the barrier.

"Shania!" he choked, his voice cracking.

His legs buckled, and he sank to the floor, his hand sliding down the glass. Shania grew smaller and smaller until the thick, external walls of the Time Gates obscured her entirely.

The ship entered the tunnel, accelerating toward the void of space. The hum of the engines was the only sound, deafening in its emptiness.

Vandar leaned back against the console behind him, his arms limp at his sides, his body a discarded marionette. He stared blankly ahead, his chest heaving as he struggled to process what had just happened.

"Shania," he whispered hoarsely, his voice barely audible. "Why have you left me here? What am I to do in this prison you've made for me?"

The words broke something inside him. Hot tears streamed down his face as his anguish spilled over, uncontained.

He wept bitterly, his sobs echoing through the empty cockpit. His worst fears had come to life—his daughter was walking into danger, and he was powerless to stop it.

<h1 style="text-align:center">52</h1>

Shania took a deep breath, steadying herself. Her heartbeat slowed, her focus sharpening into a razor's edge. The platform was empty now, the ship gone, leaving her alone with the mission she could not fail.

She slipped into the shadows, her movements silent and deliberate. Each step brought her closer to her prey.

The gangway opened into a vast hall, its stone and marble walls towering around her, oppressive in their grandeur. Shields, flags, and royal insignias hung proudly, proclaiming the lineage of the Kaldros. Above the gothic arches, stone warriors and nobles glared down at her, their faces carved with stern disdain.

She stayed close to the darkness, her footsteps ghosting along the arcade's arches. The flickering torchlight revealed Carnos guards in the gallery above, their gleaming armor making them appear more like monstrous statues than men.

Motionless and unyielding, they clutched long spears at their sides, their eyes scanning the hall below with a predator's focus.

Still, but deadly, she thought grimly, her body tensing.

The guards overlooked the main walkway leading to the central globe. If she was to pass unnoticed, she would need to move with more stealth than a whisper.

The grandeur of the hall was not lost on her, even in her tense state. The sculpted stone and marble seemed to echo with the weight of history. Above the arches, the ancestors of the Kaldros stood immortalized in statues—noble warriors and conquerors frozen in their rise to ultimate power.

Shania reached the doorway to the globe and paused. The opening loomed ahead, wide and exposed. Her pulse quickened as she assessed the situation.

Suddenly, the air around her rumbled. The walls of the Time Gates groaned under immense pressure. Looking up, she saw Horus, its monstrous gravity bending the structure around it. The spinning towers above moved in a slow, hypnotic rhythm, their jagged forms rotating over the yawning maw of the black hole.

A blinding flash of light erupted overhead, followed by a deep, resonant rumble. The first bolt of blue lightning struck the towers, illuminating the hall in a ghostly glow.

"It's beginning," Shania whispered, her voice barely audible.

She glanced at the Carnos. They didn't so much as flinch. The sound of the heavens cracking open meant nothing to them; their discipline was absolute. They remained at their posts, eyes fixed on their duty.

At the far end of the hall, a lone Carnos stood in the gallery, his figure barely visible in the dim light. Shania closed her eyes and concentrated, her thoughts honing in on the dagger strapped to his leg.

The silence in the hall was oppressive, heavy with tension. Then, with a sharp metallic clang, the dagger fell to the floor.

The sound shattered the quiet, echoing through the chamber like a gunshot.

The other Carnos reacted instantly, their statuesque stillness giving way to precise, fluid motion. They converged on the disturbance, their spears raised, their eyes searching for the intruder.

Shania seized the moment, slipping across the threshold into the heart of the Time Gates. Her steps were light as air, her movements calculated and deliberate.

Behind her, the shamed Carnos stared at his fallen dagger in dismay. Another approached, retrieving it with solemn disappointment. Without a word, he returned it to his companion, the silent exchange carrying an unspoken reprimand.

The others dispersed, returning to their posts. Order was restored, and the hall returned to its solemn glory as the heavens above continued to rumble and thunder.

Shania crouched in the shadows of the globe's entrance, her breathing steady. The first step was complete. Ahead lay the globe—and with it, the heart of the Kaldros's power, and her reckoning.

53

Vandar lay slumped on the floor, propped up by one arm. His body was still apart from the occasional twitch, and his face was pale, streaked with dried tears. His hair clung to his damp forehead, and his bloodshot eyes stared blankly at the ground.

For minutes, he didn't move. Then, with a strained breath, he pushed himself upright, each motion heavy with exhaustion. He staggered to the pilot's console and pressed a few buttons with trembling hands. Nothing happened. The controls were dead.

Vandar leaned against the edge of the console, his head bowed, and closed his eyes. Despair and helplessness clawed at him, dragging him deeper into regret.

The console bleeped. Twice.

Vandar froze, his breath catching. A third bleep followed, louder, slicing through the silence like an alarm. His head snapped up, and he turned toward the screen.

The display flickered, a series of data streams scrolling across it. His brow furrowed as he watched the ship's coordinates shift. The trajectory changed, and the vessel leaned slightly, adjusting its flight path.

"Please take positions for light travel," the ship's computer announced in a flat, unfeeling voice.

Vandar stared at the screen, his exhaustion momentarily forgotten. "Light travel?" he muttered.

Leaning closer, he squinted at the text appearing on the display:

To: Royal Flagship...

COMMAND RECEIVED: Immediate Recall - Prince Sorrell.

Returning THIS Craft to:

Guild of Earth: Radithor Palace.

The words slammed into him like a physical blow.

"Radithor Palace..." Vandar whispered, his stomach knotting. His fingers tightened on the console's edge as a chill crept up his spine.

"The Kaldros's Palace," he murmured. "It's taking me straight to him."

He rubbed his eyes, willing himself to stay calm, and scanned the screen again. The message hadn't changed. The ship's course was locked, and there was nothing he could do to stop it.

"This wasn't part of Shania's plan," he thought bitterly, his chest tightening.

But now, it was too late.

54

The yearly jolt of restorative history that would ripple through Earth and the heavens was only twenty minutes away. Shania stepped lightly along the narrow walkway in the center of the giant glass globe, her movements precise and deliberate. Ilores was near—she could feel it in the suffocating chill that clung to her skin, a hollow coldness that pressed against her very soul.

Her heart simmered with rage, stoked by thoughts of Ilores' crimes: his desecration of the universe and his betrayal of Tralonu ek Busca. Her hand tightened on the hilt of her sword as she unsheathed it, holding the blade ready. She scanned the walkways above and the metal structures below, her sharp eyes searching for any sign of the silver figure.

Shania paused, closing her eyes to focus. She could feel the energy of the Gates—alien and consuming, gnawing at the balance of the galaxy and the fragile harmony within her own being. Her breath caught as she sensed the Kaldros take his throne. Even the machine with a human mind—the invincible ruler of a thousand years—felt vulnerable in this moment, as if shedding his hardened shell like a crab.

For an instant, her composure wavered. The weight of the Kaldros's presence settled over her, oppressive and dark, a black void of foreboding.

She forced herself to open her eyes. Ilores was close.

Her pulse quickened as she moved forward silently. Then she saw him.

He stood at the railing ahead, long purple robes flowing like shadows, his silver form motionless. His head was tilted slightly upward as though counting the stars. Shania's focus narrowed, her vision tunneling to the figure before her.

Above, Horus loomed, a monstrous void devouring the light of the stars. The jagged towers of the Time Gates spun in slow, deliberate arcs, poised to harness the immense power of the black hole. A flash of blue lightning tore through the darkness, striking the towers with a deafening rumble that echoed across the glass walls.

Ilores raised his arms toward the heavens, his voice booming through the globe.

"Come! Give your strength to the Kaldros you have put in service. Come and bend the galaxy to our will!"

Shania's grip tightened around her sword as she lowered into a ready stance, her father's training steadying her movements.

"How can you ask favors of something you will never truly understand?" she called, her voice cutting through the air like a blade.

Ilores did not turn immediately. For a long moment, he remained still, taking in her words. Then, slowly, he turned his head.

"I felt your presence, girl," he said, his voice calm, almost mocking. "Long before you spoke."

Shania took a step closer, her gaze locked on his sculpted silver face. "Your ability to lie hasn't improved, Ilores. Not even after nine hundred years."

His tone sharpened. "You are no threat to me. You will fall like all the others before you."

Sweeping his cloak behind his shoulders, Ilores revealed his silver-armored body. Shania glanced briefly at the looming Horus before turning her focus back to him.

"Who are you," she said, her voice unyielding, "to speak of things so great while claiming to know more than the one who gathered the knowledge you've twisted?"

Her movements were fluid and deliberate as she shifted her stance, her sword spinning lightly in her hand.

"I am sent by the order of the traveler," she continued. "The one who journeyed across the stars and learned the truths you've corrupted."

Ilores reached behind his back, producing two orbs that glowed with molten, fiery light.

"You think the insights of Tralonu ek Busca are reserved for his pitiful disciples?" he growled. "I have seen the future. I am knowledge. I am this galaxy, and her destiny bends to my will!"

Shania shook her head, her expression almost pitying. "No. The traveler told you nothing of the future," she said softly. "And he never told you he would have children."

"Children?" Ilores laughed, his voice laced with derision.

Shania raised her sword into a defensive stance, poised for a riposte.

Ilores' growl deepened as the orbs ignited into flaming comets. He rose into the air, the burning spheres orbiting him like fiery planets.

"Many believed it was the Kaldros who taught the Carnos to fight —but it was I, Ilores!" he roared. "Now, you die!"

The orbs shot toward her, streaking through the air like vengeful stars. Shania leapt forward, twisting between them in a blur of motion. She landed lightly, her eyes tracking the orbs as they veered back for another attack.

The first orb flew past, but the second came too close. With a sharp arc of her sword, she split it cleanly in two. The molten fragments spiraled downward, vanishing into the depths of the dome.

Ilores screamed, the remaining orb circling back. He descended swiftly, the orb trailing ahead of him like a flaming sentinel.

Shania hurled her sword with precision, deflecting the orb with a loud crack. Sparks and molten debris rained down as her blade clattered to the platform.

Before she could recover it, Ilores closed the distance. She leapt into the air, manipulating gravity to meet him mid-flight. They clashed in a storm of punches and kicks, her attacks deflected by his silver limbs.

Finally, Ilores caught her leg, spinning her toward the dome wall.

She hit the glass with a sickening crack, her blood smearing the surface. Dazed, she stared at the hairline fractures spreading beneath her. The vacuum of space loomed just beyond the fragile barrier.

Pushing off the dome's metal skeleton, she launched herself toward Ilores, screaming fiercely. Her body spun mid-air, delivering a powerful kick to his head.

Ilores tumbled across the globe, slamming into a metal wall with a reverberating thud.

Shania landed on the platform, adjusting gravity and bending her knees to absorb the impact. She crouched low, gasping for breath.

The sound of footsteps echoed through the hall. She turned to see a mass of Carnos charging toward the entrance, their long spears gleaming in the dim light.

Her grip tightened on her sword as they crossed the threshold. She moved swiftly, striking where she could, severing limbs and stabbing deeply. But there were too many.

Across the platform, Ilores stood tall, his cold smile unbroken as he watched her struggle.

"How can I get out of this?" she wondered desperately.

55

Vandar stared at the console, the screen's glow flickering in the dim light. It bleeped, sharp and mechanical, and a message appeared:

'Approaching destination—dropping to sub-light speed.'

The words felt like a countdown to his doom.

Without a second thought, Vandar leapt from the pilot's seat and ran into the bowels of the ship. His footsteps echoed as he made his way to the engine room.

He stopped at the far wall where a metal panel had been pulled away earlier, revealing the black electronic unit he had been working on. Grabbing the heavy tool he'd left on the floor, he raised it high and smashed it into the device with all his strength. The box crumpled under the blow, sparks flying in every direction.

The ship shuddered violently, alarms blaring in response. The deep rumble of the engines reverberated through the hull as the ship swayed from side to side. Vandar staggered, but he pushed forward, scrambling back to the flight deck.

The thrusters roared to life, the force throwing him off balance. He barely managed to drag himself into the pilot's seat, his hands gripping the console.

He wiped his brow, heart racing, as the display flickered to show:

'Gravatis Failure: Thrusters Engaged.'

Vandar smiled grimly. He'd done it—for now.

The ship descended into Earth's atmosphere, its flight path

heading straight for the Kaldros's palace. The Prince's ship had already docked, its automated journey complete. Vandar watched as the air pressure in the docking area stabilized, preparing for the Carnos to board.

"They'll be inside in moments," he muttered.

He had already searched the entire ship for weapons, but there was nothing. All he had left was the sword he had brought from Earth. Gripping it tightly, he stood by the door, waiting for the inevitable.

The sound of boots thudding on the metal floor grew louder. Vandar' grip tightened around the hilt of his sword as the doors parted slowly.

Without hesitation, he lunged forward, his blade flashing through the air. The first Carnos guard didn't even have time to react before his head was severed in one swift motion.

The others behind him hesitated, momentarily stunned. Vandar didn't wait. He moved with lightning speed, slashing at their armor. One Carnos dropped, clutching his mangled arm, while another stumbled back, bleeding from a deep chest wound.

But there were too many.

Vandar was quickly overwhelmed. The Carnos regrouped, their spears darting out in unison. A strike to his side sent his sword spinning from his hands, and before he could react, a crushing blow knocked him to the ground.

"Damn you!" Vandar roared, struggling to break free.

They pinned him down, twisting his arms behind his back and locking metal cuffs around his wrists.

The squadron leader stepped forward, his voice deep and rasping as he spoke into his helmet intercom.

"Search the ship for the Prince."

Several Carnos moved past Vandar, their boots echoing as they stormed into the ship. Vandar gasped, his body wracked with pain, as his captors pressed him further into the dock's surface.

One of them kicked him in the chest. Vandar rolled onto his side, winded and desperate, his chest burning with agony.

A minute later, one of the Carnos returned, saluting his leader.

"The ship is empty, sir."

The squadron leader raised a hand to his helmet, listening to a message. His cold gaze shifted to Vandar, still gasping for breath on the floor.

"Take the prisoner before the Kaldros," he ordered.

Two Carnos dragged Vandar to his feet, their grip unrelenting. He struggled, but his strength had already begun to fade.

The leader turned and began walking toward the palace. The Carnos followed, dragging Vandar behind them.

56

The journey through the palace was a blur. Vandar heard the heavy iron gates creak open, the hydraulic hiss of metal doors sliding shut. The kick to his chest had winded him badly, but as they neared the Royal throne room, he began to recover, though fear still gnawed at his insides.

The palace was immense. The hallways stretched endlessly, the pillars taller than any tree. The rooms were vast, geometric in shape, with arches, vaults, and domes decorating every corner.

When he was finally brought before the Kaldros, the cold air hit him sharply as the enormous double doors—the height of three men— opened. The throne room stretched endlessly before him, the stone floor lined with mosaics of marble and mother-of-pearl.

The walkway leading up to the throne was flanked by an abyss on each side, the depths obscured by darkness. At intervals, small bridges spanned the gaps, guarded by eight silent Carnos, their presence like statues.

Vandar was dropped heavily near the foot of a short row of ascending stairs—the very stairs that led to the Kaldros's throne.

"Remove his handcuffs," the squadron leader commanded.

The guards yanked the cuffs from his wrists roughly, and Vandar immediately rubbed his raw skin, trying to regain some feeling. His legs buckled, and he dropped to his knees, looking up.

The sight before him made his heart race with dread.

The Kaldros sat upon his throne, an abomination of darkness and metal. His body gleamed black, a gruesome sheen like cold steel, his eyes glowing from yellow to blood-red. A red cape cascaded from his shoulders, nearly touching the floor. His expression was one of eternal hatred, his features carved into a frozen mask of malice.

For a moment, the Kaldros could almost be mistaken for a statue — a warning of wrath incarnate. But he was no statue.

The Kaldros's crown, more a helmet than a symbol, rose from his head like three cruel horns. On his right side, his sword was embedded halfway into the stone floor — a broad, brutal weapon.

He leaned forward, eyes narrowing as he looked down at Vandar.

"How did you come to be on my son's ship?" His voice, deep and rasping, cut through the room like a blade.

Vandar hesitated. His throat felt tight, and his body was frozen with fear. His mind spun, searching for an answer, but nothing came.

"Answer your Kaldros!" the creature bellowed, his voice like thunder.

Vandar lowered his gaze, unable to meet the Kaldros's piercing eyes. He caught sight of his sword, still sheathed near his side. He closed his eyes briefly, remembering Shania, Theresa, Tralonu ek Busca.

When he opened them again, he forced himself to look up at the Kaldros.

"I have been sent by Tralonu ek Busca — to free the universe from your shameful rule," he said, his voice trembling but resolute.

The Kaldros stood, his rage palpable. The Carnos behind Vandar shifted uncomfortably, but they did not intervene.

The Kaldros's metal arm extended, and he pointed a claw-like finger at Vandar.

"Where did you hear that name?" he demanded, his voice burning with fury.

"You and Ilores murdered him," Vandar said quietly. "But his spirit remains, passed down to my family through an object of his."

"And where is this possession?" the Kaldros sneered.

"It is bequeathed to my daughter," Vandar replied, his voice almost a whisper, as he dropped his head in silent prayer.

The Kaldros laughed — a low, guttural sound that echoed in the throne room.

"So you wish to kill me, do you?" The Kaldros removed his cape, letting it fall to the floor with a heavy thud. "Then I shall grant you an opportunity."

The squadron leader stepped back, and the doors closed with a finality that left Vandar alone with the Kaldros.

The Kaldros's Royal Guards remained at their posts, watching from the ends of the bridges.

Vandar moved back slowly, step by step, as the Kaldros descended the stairs and approached him, drawing his sword from the stone.

Vandar drew his own blade and held it before him. "Guide my sword, and my heart, Tralonu ek Busca," he whispered.

The Kaldros was a sight to behold—his body a mass of black metal, heavy yet silent in his movements. He shifted the sword with practiced ease, both defensive and offensive gestures, his joints clicking into place. Vandar tried to focus, his instincts kicking in, knowing he would need all his skill to survive.

"The length of this room may seem long, but your space will quickly be robbed," the Kaldros said, his voice a cold warning.

Vandar glanced behind him and saw the distant entry doors. If he miscalculated his movements, they could trap him.

"Each time you retreat, your space shrinks," the Kaldros continued. "When you reach the doors, they will lock, and you will be trapped. You have only four bridges to cross—don't waste your space."

The Kaldros raised his mighty arm and swung at Vandar. The blades clashed with a deafening ring. The force of the blow sent Vandar stumbling dangerously close to the edge. He regained his balance, stepping back to the center.

The Kaldros laughed, his eyes gleaming. They continued their dance, the steps growing more intense with each clash of steel. Vandar parried the Kaldros's attacks, but he was on the defensive, unable to land a blow.

He spun his blade under the Kaldros's, bringing the hilt up into his chin. The Kaldros staggered back briefly, but then retaliated with a powerful roundhouse kick to Vandar' stomach. Vandar hit the floor hard, the wind knocked from his lungs.

The Kaldros lunged toward him, sword raised high. Vandar rolled backward, narrowly avoiding the blow, and quickly regained his footing. He caught the Kaldros's sword with his own and attempted a forward kick, but the Kaldros's grip was like iron.

The Kaldros threw Vandar down again.

Vandar scrambled to his feet, his breath ragged, sweat pouring down his face. He had to move faster.

The Kaldros glanced at the first bridge to his side, and his voice rang out again.

"This is the first bridge," he said grimly.

Vandar, his body soaked in sweat and blood, readied himself for the next round of strikes.

The battle intensified. The Kaldros's blows were powerful, his strength overwhelming, but Vandar' agility began to shine through. He danced around the Kaldros's attacks, looking for an opening.

With a quick flick of his sword, Vandar slashed the Kaldros's chin, cutting through the metal edge of his faceplate. The Kaldros roared in fury, swinging back with even more force.

Vandar parried the blow, but the Kaldros's strike grazed his arm, the wound opening deep. Blood poured from the cut, but Vandar ignored the pain.

"The second bridge," the Kaldros muttered, eyeing the distance.

Vandar, weakened but determined, fought back with every ounce of strength he had left. They continued exchanging blows, each strike a test of endurance and will.

But then, the Kaldros saw the third bridge.

With a triumphant laugh, the Kaldros charged at Vandar. His strikes were relentless, and Vandar found himself struggling to defend against the onslaught.

Finally, the Kaldros raised his sword high, preparing to deliver a killing blow. Vandar saw his chance. He slashed the Kaldros's chest with a powerful strike, but the Kaldros retaliated, thrusting forward with his sword, catching Vandar' forearm.

Vandar stumbled back, his blood soaking his clothes. He could feel his strength fading.

The Kaldros stepped back, surprised at the wound, but his eyes burned with renewed rage.

Vandar, barely standing, reached for his sword with trembling hands. He tied a torn piece of cloth around his wound, knowing it wouldn't be enough.

But there was no time for hesitation.

"Your time has come, mortal," the Kaldros growled, raising his sword again.

Vandar struggled to stay on his feet. He was weak, but his heart burned with defiance. He raised his sword, feeling the weight of his final stand.

"Come and take me," Vandar challenged.

The Kaldros roared, charging forward with a high, brutal strike. Vandar blocked the attack with all his strength, and with a swift movement, he flicked his sword down toward the Kaldros's neck.

The Kaldros howled in agony, but he did not falter. He charged again, pushing Vandar to the ground, his sword pressed against Vandar' throat.

Vandar could feel the Kaldros's weight above him, the cold metal pressing into his neck.

"Tell Tralonu ek Busca to go to hell when you see him," the Kaldros sneered.

Vandar gasped, his throat constricted, but his heart was filled with rage. It wasn't over yet.

57

Shania's blade cleaved through the Carnos guard's neck, but before his head even hit the ground, the next wave of Carnos descended from the galleries above, surrounding her from all sides. She twisted and dodged, her body moving fluidly, but their relentless assault kept her on the defensive.

The Great Hall loomed around her, its towering statues of legendary warriors casting long shadows. But there was no time to admire them now.

She reached out with her mind, manipulating the gravity above the cornices and transverse arches. Rathode's statue, once a symbol of Carnos pride, began to crack. Pieces fell with a deafening rumble, shifting toward the entrance to the Time Gates.

The sound of breaking stone echoed, a warning too late for the approaching guards. One Carnos turned just in time to be pummeled by debris. His scream was cut short as the statue crushed him beneath its weight.

Shania rolled across the floor, narrowly avoiding another attack from the remaining guards. The impact of Rathode's fall threw the others off balance. Some were flung from the platform, plummeting to their deaths below.

Ilores, caught off guard, fell to the platform, sliding over the railing. He caught the support beam, halting his fall.

Shania regained her footing and counted five remaining Carnos.

With grim resolve, she leaped into the air, targeting the nearest two. The first was sent flying off the platform with a powerful kick. She landed lightly, spun, and swept her blade at the second. The Carnos guard activated his Gravatis unit, flipping over her strike and flying backward.

Frustration bubbled up inside her as she watched him retreat, always just out of reach.

But the next guard caught her off guard. His spear ripped through the back of her uniform, sending her spinning violently to one side. She turned just in time to see him diving toward her, dagger in hand. His metal-covered fist struck her face with brutal force.

Blood filled her mouth as she hit the ground, sliding on the blood of a fallen soldier. Pain roared through her head, but she forced her eyes open, ready for the next attack. The guard dove toward her, dagger raised high.

Summoning every ounce of power, she extended her arms, halting his dive. The guard screamed in surprise as he was lifted into the air, his body tossed upward toward the dome. He collided with the glass with a sickening crack, crumpling lifelessly against it.

Shania stood, her body weary but unbroken. She retrieved her sword and walked forward, releasing her control of gravity. The guard fell back to the ground behind her with a sickening thud, but she didn't flinch.

A second Carnos guard, retreating to gather his orbs, returned to the fray, flames radiating from them. Shania saw Ilores now rising from beneath the platform, his robe discarded, revealing his gleaming metal form.

"Kill her!" he bellowed, his voice sharp and commanding.

The remaining guards exchanged glances before throwing their spears aside, pulling orbs from their belts. They readied their weapons, preparing for a final assault.

Shania closed her eyes, reaching out once more. Her mind swept across the battlefield, pulling the weapons and orbs from the fallen Carnos. Spears, daggers, shields—all floated around her in a deadly array. With a wave of her hand, she sent a barrage of spears toward the first guard.

The orbs swarmed in front of him, deflecting some of the spears, but the first spear pierced his leg, causing him to falter. A second spear struck his shoulder, then his arm, and soon they rained down on him like a monsoon.

He remained in the air as long as he could, but the final spear struck his skull. He plummeted to the depths of the lower dome, his body lifeless.

Shania turned to face the two remaining Carnos. She held her sword, her body fatigued but determined. The orbs she had summoned floated around her, their surfaces glowing with radiant heat.

The guards hesitated, exchanging a brief look. Then, with synchronized movement, they dropped their orbs onto the metal floor, turning and fleeing toward the threshold door.

Ilores, unfazed by their retreat, walked confidently toward Shania, eyeing the orbs that surrounded her. There were over thirty of them, swirling in a fiery mass.

"Very good," Ilores sneered, his voice dripping with mockery. "But it won't be enough."

He stopped ten paces away, his eyes fixed on the floating orbs. He reached his metal hand out, his fingers hovering close to one.

"You are truly sent by Tralonu ek Busca himself," Ilores mused. "He was an excellent teacher. A master."

He leaned closer to the fiery sphere, his hand just inches away from it. Suddenly, all the orbs exploded, disintegrating into clouds of dust, stone, and ash. The sound was deafening, like thunder crashing across the room.

Shania recoiled in shock, her confidence shattered. Her certainty about the battle's outcome, which had been so clear moments before, was now clouded with doubt. Her heart raced, and her arms trembled as she gripped her sword.

The dust settled slowly, coating the bodies and debris on the ground. Ilores took a spear from one of the fallen soldiers, spinning it in his hands as he sized her up.

"Now," he said, grinning, "you will learn why Tralonu ek Busca is nothing more than a forgotten memory. I control the universe now."

Shania glanced at her sword, the weight of doubt settling over her. She could see the dents, the bloodstains of warriors she had felled. She had come so far, and this fight was for something much bigger than herself—her mother, the traveler, the universe itself.

With a determined scream, she charged at Ilores, her sword raised high. He caught her strike with the side of his spear and deflected it, riposting with a brutal thrust into her ribs.

She threw her free arm at his face, knocking his head sideways, giving her just enough time to bring her blade toward his armored body. The strike slid harmlessly against his metal shell.

They paused, realizing that her sword had failed to penetrate him.

Ilores growled in frustration and knocked her back, using both hands to push the spear's length. She stumbled, but quickly regained her footing.

He spun, gathering momentum for a vicious strike. The spear's end hit her thigh, and she collapsed, her body racked with pain.

Ilores moved in, preparing to deliver the killing blow.

In a flash, Shania changed the gravity around her, sliding across the floor, away from him. He chased her, launching himself into the air with the help of Gravatis.

Shania reached the archway, her body burning with pain, but she pushed herself harder. She levitated herself just high enough to land on the wall by the archway, absorbing the impact with a deep bend in her legs.

Ilores landed further down the wall, avoiding her sword's reach. She ran along the curved wall of the globe, but Ilores was in hot pursuit.

She ran as fast as her battered body would allow, the sword slowing her down. With a sharp motion, she threw the weapon into the center of the globe, where it spun slowly, waiting for her return.

Shania leaped into the air, spiraling toward the spinning sword. Ilores followed, but Shania was already ahead. She caught the handle of the sword just in time and spun mid-air.

Ilores came into view, and she slashed the blade toward him. The sword pierced his armor with a sharp rip, severing the black unit attached to his back.

Ilores screamed in agony as he fell, helplessly plummeting to the platform below.

Shania watched him descend, her heart pounding in her chest. The battle was far from over, but for the first time, she felt hope rise within her.

58

Shania's relief was indescribable—she felt the weight of justice fulfilled. She lowered herself painfully to the ground beside the dead man, exhaustion sweeping over her. Her eyes closed. Above, between Horus and the Time Gates, the air rumbled as the towering blades moved in the wake of Horus' spiraling mouth. Occasionally, the dark space lit with flickers of energy, bolts of lightning tearing between the Time Gates and the black hole.

But then, an unsettling feeling crept over her—nausea building from deep inside, a sixth sense of impending danger. Her heart quickened.

She snapped her eyes open, the sound of thunder and lightning growing louder. The energy from Horus began striking the Time Gates with brutal force.

Suddenly, she shot upright, panic flooding her chest as she yelled out:

"Father!"

She leapt to her feet, hand pressed to her head as if to push away the horrible premonition. Her father—somewhere—was in danger. She bolted toward the fallen statue of Rathode, heading for the gap she could slip through to return to the hangar—where the ships were.

The Time Gates rumbled again, this time with an earth-shattering force, knocking her off balance. The sky above the globe lit with massive electrical arcs—energy crackling out from Horus' mouth and slamming into the towers of the Time Gates. The whole place was engulfed in a storm of blue electricity.

The Time Gates were coming to life with the energy of The Quantisation.

Shania stood, unsteady on the shaking floor, but she forced herself forward.

She had to find her father, and somehow stop The Quantisation. Time was running out for both.

The ground trembled violently, shaking like an earthquake, as she pushed through the Great Hall. She was nearing the gangway back to the hangar when a red glow from a doorway to her left caught her eye.

For a moment, she hesitated—glancing from the ships in the hangar to the room bathed in eerie red light. Something deep inside her compelled her to move toward it.

She stepped forward cautiously, entering the room.

Immediately, two Carnos, stationed inside, attacked.

Shania reacted instantly, using her legs to deliver powerful kicks, followed by helmet-crushing punches. The two guards collapsed against the stone wall, sliding to the floor, unconscious.

She stepped deeper into the amber-red glow, heart racing.

The room was filled with angled walls and shifting spaces. Stones rotated on moving circles and eclipses, spinning in unending cycles. Pillars rose and fell at specific intervals, carved with strange symbols. It was like a living chessboard, gears grinding, weights shifting. The air was thick with the smell of oil and burning fuel.

Shania stood still, trying to process it all. This place... it was familiar.

At the center, a circle with a symbol caught her eye. The same symbol glowed on her wristband—the gift from Tralonu ek Busca.

Her heart skipped a beat. She realized the function of the room.

This was the Time Gates' Gravatis.

Shania's mind raced as she walked around the room, her heart pounding in her chest. She had stumbled upon the very heart of the Kaldros's control over the universe—the source of his power.

She reached out, her fingers brushing against one of the heaviest stones.

With a resounding crack, the stone shifted, breaking free from its orbit in the intricate design. It collided with other pieces, sending shockwaves through the machine. A violent tremor shook the entire structure, as the sound of shattering stone echoed like the death knell of the Kaldros's control.

Shania's breath caught as she turned and sprinted from the room. The machine ground to a halt, and dust and debris filled the air as the room trembled from the impact.

She didn't look back as she raced toward the gangway, the sound of crumbling stone urging her on as she stumbled toward the hangar.

59

The station erupted into chaos—alarms shrieked, Carnos scrambled in every direction, some knocking into each other in panic as they rushed toward the ships. The air was thick with confusion and fear.

Shania darted through the confusion, throwing a Carnos pilot aside as she leaped into the cockpit. Her hands shot to the controls, her mind racing. With a surge of willpower, she wrenched the ship free, feeling the cold metal of the cockpit as it responded to her command.

The silver ship blasted from the Time Gates just as the massive arcs of electricity tore through the machine. The Time Gates groaned, the resistance against the black hole faltering. One tower sheared off in a burst of sparks, disappearing into the abyss. The lights of the machine flickered, then died as it was drawn toward its doom. In less than a second, the Time Gates were no more.

Shania punched the ship into light speed. Her heart hammered in her chest as the stars stretched out before her. She prayed she would find her father in time—but deep inside, a cold truth gnawed at her. He was already slipping away. Lost somewhere in time. She was too late.

<h1 style="text-align:center">60</h1>

Vandar tried to push the Kaldros's blade away, but his attempts were futile. The Kaldros's weight, the full force of his metal bulk, pressed down with crushing power. Vandar's face flushed, growing red, then blue. His ears rang with the force of the pressure, and his lungs screamed for air. His muscles weakened, his body tiring, as each moment without breath felt like an eternity.

He felt his strength slipping away. The world narrowed, his vision dimming. Every cell in his body cried out for air, a suffocating, desperate need worse than pain. His mouth opened and closed in pitiful gasps—like a dying fish. His body thrashed, struggling to clear the block in his throat, but his efforts grew weaker, more frantic. He felt himself slipping, his eyelids growing heavy, pulling him toward an endless sleep.

Then, a rattle.

A piece of metal clattered to the floor. For the briefest moment, the Kaldros's push lessened. Vandar gasped, filling his lungs with air, his chest heaving. He opened his eyes, trembling, and saw the Kaldros's armor—piece by piece—falling away.

The Kaldros faltered, his iron grip slipping from the hilt of the sword. The blade clattered free, leaving Vandar with a hard-won breath.

The Kaldros stumbled back, clutching his shoulders as his body slowly began to disassemble. Metal popped off with sickening sounds, the pieces clattering to the floor like discarded refuse. The crown's three sharp points fell to the ground, ringing out across the tiles, their weight suddenly insignificant.

"What's happening to me?" the Kaldros rasped, lifting his arm. But instead of muscle, he watched in horror as his metal bones twisted and unraveled. The armor fell away in pieces, revealing a bloodied, disintegrating human torso—what remained of the once-immortal Kaldros. His skull cracked open, the top half peeling away like old bark, leaving only the barest human remnants.

Vandar recoiled in terror as the human flesh and bone twisted and writhed, as if fighting to remain whole—an agonizing dance of decay, the last remnants of the Kaldros's twisted existence. The blood evaporated into the air, the bones hardened and cracked, and the Kaldros crumbled into dust.

Vandar screamed, dragging himself away from the remains, scattering the pieces with a violent motion. He crawled, panicked, across the floor, stumbling against the double doors, his body slick with sweat and blood. He looked back once, at the Kaldros's final, pathetic fragments. The Kaldros was gone.

He collapsed to the ground, sickened and trembling. He rolled over and vomited, his stomach churning with the weight of it all.

The Carnos stepped forward, slowly, watching him. Their silence was deafening. The leader of the Carnos stepped forward, his movements slow and deliberate. His cape fluttered like a flag, torn between loyalty and something darker. He dropped his sword onto the floor with a heavy thud, and one by one, the others followed suit, throwing down their weapons.

Without a word, they turned and began to leave, walking through the massive doors. The sound of their footsteps faded, leaving Vandar alone in the silent, empty Throne Room. The doors creaked shut behind them, and Vandar was left, breathing hard, his chest heaving with the remnants of his panic.

Barely a minute passed before the doors opened again. Soft footsteps echoed across the floor. Vandar's heart leaped.

"Shania!" he gasped.

She turned to him, and the light in her eyes brought him to life. She ran to him, her arms open, and they collided in an embrace so fierce it felt like it could break the world. Tears streamed down both their faces, mingling with the blood and sweat of battle.

"I love you," Vandar whispered into her hair.

"Oh, Dad," she murmured, her voice thick with emotion. "I thought I'd lost you."

He pulled back, his hands gently tracing her face, memorizing every inch of her. "Lost me?" he smiled. "Don't count on it."

He hugged her again, tight, as if trying to hold the whole universe in that one moment.

"How did you survive?" she asked, her voice full of awe.

Vandar looked at her, bewildered. "I was fighting the Kaldros, and then he... crumpled. Vanished."

Her face lit up with a knowing smile. "You destroyed the Gravatis device, didn't you?"

"I did," Vandar said, still processing everything. "I hoped I'd be far enough in the future—or past—not to see him again."

Shania laughed, a sound of relief. "Well, lucky for you, it took you to the future. I came from the past to find you here, almost a hundred years ahead of me."

Her grin widened. "I killed Ilores."

Vandar's eyes widened in disbelief. "You did?"

He paused, letting the weight of it sink in. "So the Kaldros was doomed."

She nodded solemnly. "He couldn't survive without Ilores to keep him alive."

Vandar smiled, a warm, genuine smile. "You saved me."

"No," Shania whispered, her voice tender, "you've been saving me since I was born. We're a team."

Vandar chuckled, the tension draining from his body.

"A real family," he said, shaking his head in wonder.

They stood there for a moment, just holding each other, feeling the weight of everything they had been through.

"It's a funny thing, time travel," Vandar mused, looking at the ruins of the Throne Room.

Shania helped him to his feet, steadying him as they walked together.

"Imagine all the places we could go..." Shania said, her voice light with possibility.

61

They stood side by side at the window of the spaceship, staring out at Horus, watching as the black hole slowly receded, slipping back into its endless orbit around the Cosmos.

Vandar gazed at the swirling chaos outside. The Time Gates were gone, leaving a vast, uncharted future behind. Stars stretched and twisted, pulled apart by the forces they could no longer control. The light from distant worlds flickered, bending under the immense pull of Horus.

What would this mean for the universe? Would it remain the same, or would they reshape it, for better or worse?

He felt the weight of it settle in. No answers—only the heavy silence of the unknown.

Shania stood beside him, her brow furrowed in thought, but she said nothing. The hum of the ship filled the air, the stars beyond nothing but distant points of light, caught between the past and an uncertain future.

"That..." Vandar said after a long pause, his voice quiet, "is for the people of the universe to decide."

The words hung in the air. The moment seemed endless, stretching into the void, as if the universe itself were waiting for its next move. No more Time Gates, no more restrictions on what could be changed. The future was as open and fragile as the stars they watched, pulsing in the distance.

And yet, in the stillness, both knew there was no turning back.
What happened next—how the universe would be shaped—was now
in the hands of those who dared to act.